T0077698

Half-Breed

Phylly Smith

Dellarte Press™
1663 Liberty Drive
Bloomington, IN 47403
www.dellartepress.com
Phone: 1-877-217-3420

First published by Dellarte Press: 2/16/2010

ISBN: 978-1-4501-0005-2 (sc)
ISBN: 978-1-4501-0004-5 (e)

Printed in the United States of America
Bloomington, Indiana

This book is printed on acid-free paper.

This book is dedicated to the lady with the amber eyes,
my mom.

And to my fellow wolves, live on.

Acknowledgements

Firstly, I thank God for all his blessings. And many, many, many thanks to my family and all my supporters. It means a lot.

Chapter 1

The house seems empty without him. I sit on my bed soaking and cold in a hand-me-down of a black dress. I kick my mud-soled boots off my feet and stare at nothing in particular. I miss him. The funeral couldn't have ended more than twenty minutes ago and I miss him, terribly. I don't want to imagine how I'll feel in an hour. And the storm is terrible. It's perfect weather for his funeral and my seventeenth birthday. I can hear slow steps and deep sobs coming up the stairs. I shift positions to lie on my stomach. The door creaks when it opens. "I...I um didn't get a chance to get a birthday cake for you." What else is new? "But there's a fruit cake Mrs. Howlman bought…" Sigh. "You should come get a slice." "That was dad's favorite cake, not mine." I press the side of my face into my pillow. "I know…it...was…his favorite." Each word seemed harder for her to say. "But I think you should come downstairs and eat and we can…talk." I sit up and look at my tearful mother. Now she wants to talk to me, after years of ignoring me and being more interested in blond-ing her hair and getting her mani-pedi's, she wants to talk to me. Quite frankly I'd rather stare into nothingness. "Talk, about what?" "I don't know…" she dabs her nose with a tissue "…

things." I sigh deeply and shrug. The steps creak as I walk downstairs. I continue to the kitchen and slide down onto an old wooden chair positioned on one side of the table, my mom on the other side looking as miserable as I do. This is definitely the picture for a perfect family dinner. I stare down at my plate of four day old leftovers. With my fork I push the rubbery chicken leg into the waxy peas. She notices. "Amelia." She says it so stern. I hate the way she says it. I wish she'd call me Lia, like dad used to. "Eat please. You need to." "I'm not hungry." Not for leftovers anyways that the dog wouldn't even eat. Her collar jingles and she pushes her leathery nose into my thigh. I tear off a strip of chicken and drop it on the floor. She sniffs and denies my offer. Just what I thought, not even the dog would eat it. "Jojo, get out." My mom demands, her finger pointing the way. "There's nothing wrong with her being in here." I hold onto Jojo's studded collar. She lets the fork clatter onto the plate, obviously upset; she doesn't even finish eating the delicious food. She takes her plate and mine, crashing them into the deep, porcelain sink, thank God they're plastic. She begins to fill the sink with water. "Amelia, I have had this discussion with you before. I barely want that retriever in the house let alone the kitchen." She submerges a sponge into the soapy water. "It's not like she's on the table or rubbing her tail all over the counter top." I retort, still holding Jojo in place. "Listen, this is my house, my rules. That damn dog will never be allowed in here if I say so." Her anger rises and water begins to splash the faster she scrubs. "Jojo is me and dad's dog, she will always be allowed." Tears choke my throat. The chair scrapes the floor as I push away and rush upstairs, Jojo follows. I pull off the dress and throw it on the floor. It's a horrible, itchy thing. We don't have time to look for a dress for you, she tells me. She never seems to have time when it comes to me. But, Mrs. Howlman has some old dresses that she sewed. How convenient. While scratching all over my body I manage to pull on an oversized t-shirt. I crawl into bed, the blankets swallow me up. Jojo lies next to me and her quiet panting is lulling. I only wish my dad was still here. I close my eyes, listening to the crackling and thundering of the storm until I fall asleep completely.

CHAPTER 2

Something's tapping me on my forehead, something wet and cool. Tap.tap. tap. Annoyed, I slowly open my eyes to see a constant trickling of water dripping from the ceiling. Sigh. I turn on my side and cover one side of my face with my hand. But the insistent drop seeps through my fingers, still managing to wet my cheek. It forces me to get up. Jojo's already gone. Maybe the leaky ceiling got to her too. I grab a small plastic basket and place it on my bed to catch the leak. I walk down the creaking staircase and almost trip over the boxes waiting at the bottom. I step over what seems hundreds of boxes to finally make it into the living room. My mom is in a head scarf and overalls, horribly singing her heart out. Great, time to unpack. I call to her, she doesn't answer. "Mom!" I cup my mouth with both hands. She keeps singing off –key while she pulls dusty trinkets out of a box. I tap her on the shoulder and she jumps. "Oh, Amelia…" she pulls the small buds out of her ears "…you scared me." "Is that *my* MP3 player?" I notice the small silver device cradled in her hand. "Yeah, I needed something to listen to while I unpack." "You could have asked." I surly suggest. She exhales, puts the mini music player on a box and resumes unpacking. We moved here only four weeks ago. Dad wanted to, he claimed it would help with his writing. He said this place was full of wonder and excitement when he lived here as a boy. Looking around at the aged torn wallpaper, the leaky roof, and creaking loose floorboards proves opposite to his description. *A little elbow grease,* he would say, *is all the place is going to need.* We're going to definitely need more than elbow grease. "Oh, Amelia, call Mrs. Howlman and thank her for the dress it was nice of her to give to you." She dusts off a small crystal clown and gently places it next to the rest of her clown collection. Yuck. Mrs. Howlman, our neighbor, if you can call her that. Her house is a ten minute drive from here. I know, because I was counting the clock when we had to go pick up my couture gown. She lives in a house similar to ours-- two levels, five rooms, a large front porch, and a bigger back porch. That day she offered us tea and crunchy cookies that too closely resembled dog biscuits. We should have brought Jojo. Mom pushed me in my back forcing me to partake in either a cup of tea or a dog biscuit. I chose tea. "I knew your father when he was a little boy all the way until he moved away when he was about your age, such a sweet young man." Her spotted hand trembles as she brings the rim of the cup closer to her lips. "And he just adored my fruitcakes." Her wrinkled mouth forms a smile. Mom smiled softly and acted like she was enjoying this get together. "You know dear, you look just like him, especially those eyes. He was quite handsome." Oh great, just what a girl wants to hear, she's handsome. To be polite, I forced a smile. Twenty minutes and four forced smiles later she slowly made her way downstairs and back to the living room, with a shapeless, old, ugly dress. "Here you are, dear." She laid the dress across my lap. "Thanks Mrs. Howlman" is all I could manage. "Amelia?" My mom is adjusting her head scarf with a questioning look on her face, "what are you thinking about?" I shake away weeks old memories. "Oh, nothing, I just can't remember her number. Maybe I'll mail her a thank you note."

I lean against the wall. "Dear Mrs. Howlman, thank you for giving me the itchiest and probably the ugliest dress ever." My mom sighs sharply and grabs her purse from the kitchen table. "If you had agreed to a dress or two when I offered to buy them for you we wouldn't have had that problem. No, all you wanted was skinny jeans, too-tight tank tops, and more skinny jeans." She pulls a wrinkled strip of paper from the bottom of her purse. "Start dialing." I take it, begrudgingly. I disconnect my cell from its charger on the counter, flip open the screen, and no reception. Of course there isn't. I walk through various parts of the house with my phone held in the air, waiting to see bars of life. When I reach the back porch I get two flickering bars of reception. I don't want to call. Sigh. Just get it over with. I dial and impatiently wait through ring after ring. She answers. Damn, I was hoping for an answering machine. "Good morning, Mrs. Howlman." "Oh, dear! How are you?" Her cheeriness scares me. "I'm fine. I just wanted to thank you for giving me that dress to wear." "You're very welcome. You looked so beautiful in it on such a sad day." You've got to be kidding me. "I'm going to have my grandson bring you two more dresses. I figure you can wear these on happier days." She's smiling, I can tell. Before I can refuse her offer she says to tell my mother she said hello and hangs up. My mom comes from behind and grabs my arm. I jump. "Scare you?" Her smile grows wide. "No, you didn't." I caress my elbow, trying to mask my brief moment of fright. "Did you really have to grab me? I think I bruised." "Amelia, you're such a drama queen. Anyways, what'd she say?" "Hello to you and that she's sending her grandson by to bring me more of her beautiful original dresses." I mimic Mrs. Howlman's voice and roll my eyes. "That is so sweet." My mom squeezes my shoulder. "And you said her grandson is bringing them?" she lifts her eyebrow and smiles. "Mom, please." "What? It will be a good chance for you to get to know someone here who might be you age." As if I want to. She recognizes my disinterest. "Well at least go and change out of your pajamas, if he's coming you could at least look like you care." Sigh.

CHAPTER 3

I don't like this house. It's smelly, creaky, and dreary. Matter-of-fact I don't like Wolf Falls. This town matches this house. It's always gray weather, cloudy, and windy. The outside air smells like wet dog and it makes me nauseous. Ugh. I'm out of my pajamas per my mom's request. I put on a pair of skinny jeans, a white tank, and a hoodie. Now the only thing left to do is my hair-- a task I never look forward to. I try to comb through my sandy tinted wildness. It's a mess of hair that stops just past the middle of my back. Some have called it nice, like my mom's friends, Bunny and what was the other one's name, Muffy or Muffin; I don't know it was something like that. They would smile really tight and touch my hair with their fingertips. "Her hair is pretty Joan; I mean it doesn't seem *that* nap-…tangled." Bunny quickly caught herself. "Uh, yes, it is, believe me, she broke two combs." Mom would laugh with her friends while they all sipped their blood-colored wine. Ever since that, I had a dislike for my hair. It's tangled and messy. My mom never knew what to do with it. Being white, her straight, easy-to-comb hair was never a problem. But growing up with a half black daughter proved challenging for her. It was a challenge for me too, my hair never seemed combed. Luckily, in fifth grade, I went to my friend's sleepover and her mother was giving all us girls' fun hairstyles. When it was my turn, she used this oil that smelled so good and sweet. She rubbed it from my roots to the tips and my hair was glossy and all waves. And more importantly I could comb through it. Ever since that I've begged my mom to buy that oil for me. Which she has, I have close to a crate of the stuff. I guess she was just as happy of my hair discovery as I was. I look in the mirror one last time and I do see my dad, a lot. I look at my large, brown, almond eyes, full lips and lighter auburn skin tone. I miss him. I flip the light switch and make my way downstairs, Jojo following close behind. "Look at you all prettied up." My mom smiles leaning on the kitchen counter. I smile softly. "Mom, please." I pull myself onto the other end of the counter top. "You know I really think you should start eating, because skinny jeans shouldn't make you look that-skinny." She looks at me concerned. "Ok mom, whatever you say." I stare up at the ceiling. "Anyways who can think about food when I haven't decided if I should burn them or throw them away?" I keep my stare at the ceiling. "What are you talking about?" my mom sips from her cup. "The dresses Mrs. Howlman are sending." She stops drinking and looks at me. "Be nice, she's a sweet old lady who's only trying to help." "Sure."I rub Jojo's soft coat. My mom looks out the large kitchen window. "That must be him." She coos. "What a cute-y." I turn around and look with her. He is. He's at least six feet tall, deep brown skin, close cropped hair, and a toned body. Not that I noticed. He could have been perfect if he wasn't holding those dresses. "Go, go" my mom forces me off the countertop. He rings the doorbell. When I open the door, he smiles. I smile. Why am I smiling? He's not that cute. Ok yes, he is. Still, stop smiling. "Are you Amelia?" Say something. "Oh, um yes, that's me, Amelia." He smiles again and his eyes oddly flicker to an amber then back to deep brown. "I have some dresses for you from my grandmother."

He gives me the bundled hangers. "Amelia, who do we have here?" Mom comes from the kitchen acting like she doesn't know what's going on, furthering my embarrassment. She smiles. "Hi, I'm Mrs. Brewer, Amelia's mom. But please, call me Joan." "I'm Zev." He courteously extends his hand and she takes and shakes and smiles. "What are you up to today, Zev?" She's already trying to push me off on a date. I can't believe her. I can feel myself getting irritated and once that happens I start to sweat and that definitely won't be a cute look. Just relax Lia and take a couple breaths you could be overreacting. She could just be acting courteous. "Nothing much, just going down to the pizzeria, hanging with some friends." He flashes his gleaming smile. "Oh, Amelia loves pizza!" I knew I wasn't overreacting. "Mom" I say through clenched teeth. "I have to help you finish unpacking." "It'd be cool if you came, Amelia. I could introduce you and show you around." I smile softly. How could I say no to him? I can feel Mom squeezing my forearm. "Oh, um, yea I guess that'd be okay." To mom's excitement, after I agree she rushes to her purse and back and pushes a twenty dollar bill in the pocket of my hoodie. "Do you have your cell?" she asks. "Yeah" I take it out of my pocket and make sure it's charged. "Well you two have fun, don't be home too late Amelia." She waves to me as she practically pushes us off the front porch. I have the type of mom who thinks the more dates you go on, the more friends you have, the more people you know, the better your life will be. We are so opposite. I'd think I'd still have a good life if I spend some of my teen years on the couch with a bag of chips watching cable. "So, Amelia…" he begins. "Oh, call me Lia." "Lia. I like that." Oh great, I know I'm blushing. "So, Lia, how old are you?" "I'm seventeen, you?" "Eighteen." He pushes his hands into his pockets. I start to chew on the inside of my lip. Small talk makes me nervous. "Summer should be fun." "I guess." I quietly agree-- if you call no sun and windiness, summer. I softly kick up pebbles as we walk down the gravel pathway.

"So are we walking to the pizza place?" "Not unless you like really, really long walks." He laughs softly. We stop at a classic mustang parked at the end of the walkway. It's cream-colored lacquer with bold black stripes racing up the hood all the way back down the trunk. "My dad loved classics, what year is this?" I softly rub my hand against the hood. He answers with a smile. "A '66." "It's really nice." I compliment as I slide onto the cream- colored leather upholstered seat. Actually, nice is an understatement. "How'd you get a car like this?"I look around at the flawless interior. "Lots of hard work and time, plus working nights and some weekends for the town mechanic can have its perks. When he starts the car the engine rumbles then hums, sending vibrations through my body. He takes off. Gravel and dust are left in a cloud behind us. "How are you liking Wolf Falls?" he hugs the curve of the street as he pushes the gas to eighty. "It's um alright, I don't really know yet." I push my back into the seat and grab hold of the door handle. He notices, laughs, and starts to slow down. "It's a cool place. I've been here my entire life. I know its ins and outs and secret hiding places." I release my tense position and clear my throat. "Well since you know a lot about here, how's the pizza? I know it doesn't beat New York's." I reminisce about the over-sized slices I used to eat with friends after school. "Ah, its pretty good, you'll just have to try it." He pulls into the only available space of the small parking lot. He gets out and opens my door for me-- hmm chivalrous and cute. I smile softly. The wind picks up. I zip my hoodie up and try to hold my flying hair down. He leads the way. As soon as we step into the restaurant Zev points to three people--a girl and two guys, sitting in a corner booth. They don't seem to notice us approaching. I unzip my hoodie and run my hand over my hair. "You look fine." He smiles. His smile is a killer. He grabs my hand softly. The girl in the booth notices us first. And I don't think she likes what she sees.

CHAPTER 4

The pizzeria is small with three booths, four petite tables, and a lone pinball machine in one corner. The fluorescent lighting and checkered floors seem to make the place even smaller. A few people are sitting at tables and seem heavily involved in a conversation and their pizza, until I walk in. The whispers begin. I hold onto Zev's hand tighter. It seems like the booth is stretching further and further away from us. I feel uncomfortable and I just want to sit down and make the whispers stop. Better yet, I just want to get in his classic car and drive home. Finally, we reach the booth. She stares at me, more mean than inviting, while she picks at a pepperoni stuck on her slice of pizza. "Zev, what's going on man?" A slender guy, with dangerously spiked hair, stands and greets Zev, cheerfully pulling him into a manly hug. "We got the pizza like thirty minutes ago." He looks at me. "It took you forever to get here." He says, obviously wanting to know who I am. "Yeah we were getting ready to eat without you." A darker skinned guy with thin lengthy cornrows adds. Zev smiles. "I had to go drop off some things to my new friend." He acknowledges me. "Samuel, Dante, this is Lia. She's new to the Falls." "So this is her?" Dante says. Zev and Samuel shoot him a look. "You can call me Sammy." Spiky steps forward, his strong features instantly tell me he's Native American. Dante smiles and nods to me. "And you can have the pleasure of calling me Tay." He leans forward, gently takes my hand, and kisses it. Zev pulls my hand away. "Tay, she hasn't even been here ten minutes and you're already flirting." "What can I say, she's beautiful." His eyes do a color change, like Zev's. I notice and try to look away. I can't. "Anyways" Zev ushers for me to slide into the vinyl booth. "What's up Aja?"Zev says as he slides in next to me. She flips her black silky hair behind her shoulders and I swear when she looks up her dark green eyes flicker golden. That's really starting to freak me out. "Hi Zev" I'm completely ignored as she acts as though I'm not there. "Aja Lia, Lia Aja." His quick introduction is wasted as she starts looking through her cell. Not like I care to know her. She doesn't care to know me either. Good, we're on the same level. Sammy and Tay slide in next to Aja. Zev passes me a paper plate and slides a wide long slice of pepperoni pizza on it. Already plated they start to eat their slices, in two bites. I'm amazed; these are huge slices of pizza. I pick mine up with both my hands and bite off the tip. That's all I could get in my mouth. "How's it taste, as good as New York's?" Zev wipes the corners of his mouth. "Yeah, it's pretty good." I finish the slice in small bites. "Want anymore?" Zev offers, sliding the pan towards me. "No thanks." One slice is enough for me. After the pan is finished, our booth is quiet. "Since when are *you* so quiet, Aja?" Tay leans closer to her and puts his arm around her shoulder. She pushes it off. He does it again. She pushes it off and he does it again. He's persistent. "Cut it out." She growls with flickering eyes. He laughs. "Don't be so touchy Aja." Tay moves him arm, directing his attention to a balled up napkin and throws it at Zev. She looks at Zev. He's now tossing the napkin ball between himself, Sammy, and Tay. She's staring now-- a soft, wanting look, almost…sweet. She likes him. Her eyes dart to me and I freeze. Great, she saw me staring. That's all I need, more problems. This girl already doesn't like me. "What are you looking at, half breed?" The last words stun me. I've been called it once or twice before but not since I was thirteen. It still hurts. The ballplayers stop. The napkin drops on the ground. I can feel my face getting hot and I'm getting ready to bite back when Zev interjects. "Damn, Aja why did you call her that?!" The other two just stare. "That's what she is." She says with no remorse. "I can think of a name to call you that would describe you exactly, but I don't." Bitch. Is that the name he's thinking, because that's exactly what I'm thinking. I reach for my cell-- the clock says 8:54 p.m. I am so ready to go. "Hey Zev, I should get going." I slide my body over towards him which prompts him to slide out of the booth. "Zev, remember, cabin house, in an hour." Sammy looks at us. Tay nods a good bye. He has an odd, sly look on his face. "Alright." He opens the door for me-- the little bell chimes our exit. I slide into the Mustang and slowly put the seat belt on. Zev does the same, he looks upset and embarrassed. Oh, how I love awkward silences. I chew on the inside of my lip. He pulls out and starts driving the road to my deliverance, my house. Fifteen minutes of dead silence. Maybe I should talk about the weather. I look through the windshield and see the heavy pale gray clouds. Uh, never mind. While I'm trying to think of something to say, Zev quickly looks at me and back at the road. "Hey, I'm sorry about Aja. She just doesn't know how to be nice sometimes. We don't meet a lot of new people here." He makes an excuse. "I mean she can be nice, don't get me wrong." Really, when is that? "Zev, it's cool, I've been called that before, and it doesn't hurt." Yes it does. "Okay, I just don't want your feelings to be hurt." He pulls up the pathway stopping closer to the front porch. "My feelings are ok." I smile weakly. He puts the car in park. "Don't worry about what she calls you, ok, she doesn't mean it." His concern is sweet. He slips my cell phone out of my hand, presses buttons, and returns it a minute later. "Call me whenever you want to talk or go out or something." He smiles. "I will." My heart has to be beating a thousand times per minutes. I hope I don't do something stupid. "Talk to you later?" "Sure." Be cool, Lia. Be cool. I open the door and pull forward and I'm instantly snapped back. I lean back and unbuckle myself. The seatbelt is totally against me and my attempt to be cool. I try to flash a cute smile. Hopefully it covers my embarrassment. Stupid seatbelt. I walk up the three creaking steps that lead to the front door. I unlock it, turn slightly, and wave. He waves back before taking off, leaving a dust cloud behind him. "How was it?!" Mom scares the crap out of me. "Fine" I put my hand over my heart. It was already beating fast, now it's at warp speed. Any faster and I don't think I could take it. "Did he kiss you?" "Mom!" I answer, horrified that she asked. "Tell me." she squeals. No way would I tell her, even if he did-- man, I wish he did. "It was like a hang out thing, not a date. And uh we just met earlier today. I'm not going to kiss him that fast."Jojo comes up to me. She stands on her back legs and rests her front paws on my thigh, like always. "Hey Jojo" I scratch behind her ears. After a few seconds of scratch therapy I pat her back and she goes back to all fours trotting into the living room. "So did anything interesting happen at least?" she folds her arm. I don't want to tell my mom about the name-calling, she's so shamefully sensitive about it. The first time I was called a rude name about being mixed was when I was six. My mom and I were in a grocery store and I was so excited that I was going to get these fruity-flavored swirly popsicles all I could do was stare at the brightly colored box and read the funny story on the back. So I didn't recognize when my mom left the aisle. When I noticed I was alone I started seriously freaking out and two workers, a dark-haired woman and a blonde guy, who acted really girly, tried to calm me down and asked me where my mother was. "Honey" He held my hands "don't cry. We'll find her." They lead me down two aisles, we found her on the second one. "There she is." I said through a snotty nose. And of course they lead me to the other woman down the aisle, a black woman. "Not her." I walk to my mom and try to grab her hand but she doesn't accept my offer. "*She's* your mother?" They looked at each other and my mom looked at them then down at me, her reddened face full of shame. The workers turn around and with a loud whisper he says to her "you sure can't tell those mutts, wow." I never forgot that day and I probably never will. "Amelia..." Mom waves her hands "…woo-hoo.". "No, no nothing interesting just ate pizza. I'm going to bed I'm feeling a little tired." I force a fake yawn. I think she knows it's fake. "Alright" she lifts an eyebrow. "Tomorrow you need to unpack your room. So we can put some of these boxes away." "Ok" I walk upstairs, Jojo's steadily behind me. I sit down on my bed, slide my boots off, and fall back with my arms open. I smile and think about him which makes my smile even bigger. We're just friends. I tell myself. Don't get too serious. I mean you just met the guy Lia, give it time. Yeah, give it time. I slide my cell out of my pocket and hold it in the air. The LED screen casts a blue shadow over my face. I scroll through my address book-- there it is the sixth name down, Zev. Maybe I should text him. Like something fun and cute. Night-y night. Ugh. -Sleep tight. Who am I, his mom? – Lia stop agonizing over it, just send a message so he can have your number. *I had a great time, talk to you later- Lia.* Not so fun and cute, but it's simple and to the point. I press send and sit my phone on my nightstand. The screen's glow dims as I pull off my jeans and hoodie. I crawl into bed. Jojo jumps up and stretches her body out next to me. I'm smiling still. My cheeks will definitely start to numb if I don't stop. I should sleep. I close my eyes. It might not be so bad here.

Chapter 5

I wake up the next morning in practically the same amount of light I went to sleep in. Seriously, is there ever any sun? I turn on my lamp and sit up. The barren room definitely needs some furniture and a few posters tacked here and there. It's a large space with original wood flooring and molding. It's all cherry wood, so it makes the room seem even darker. And my dream of having a walk-in closet have come true, not that I have enough clothes to fill it. But still, having it is awesome. I push back the thin covers and pull on my pajama pants I left on the floor. I start going through two boxes already sitting in a corner of my room. The first box-- a couple pillows, an extra blanket, and my clock radio. I fully make up my bed with my boxed bedding and stand my clock radio on the only vacant spot of my side table. One box down and three-thousand more boxes to go. Okay, I'm exaggerating. I sit on my bed and pull the second box close to my feet. I lift its flap to reveal me and my dad's stuff-- our own creations. We would sit for hours painting and sculpting, while my mom was out at getting her nails done or hanging out with her girlfriends. I laugh at a painting I did when I was seven. It was supposed to be me and my dad but it turned out to look more like two blobby messes with hair. But no matter how my paintings looked he always kissed my forehead and said "Perfect, Lia". Then he would attach it to the refrigerator with a magnet. I fight the oncoming tears. I shove it back in the box, close the flaps, and push it back into the corner. Depressing. It's silent for minutes until my stomach growls. I walk down the stairs and flip the lights on in the kitchen. Wow, my mom was really working yesterday. Almost everything is unpacked and in place. I go to the cabinet and pull down a box of cereal. I pour it in a plastic bowl and drown the sugary rings in milk. "Look who is up before noon." She smirks. "I was hungry." I shove a spoonful of cereal into my mouth. "I see." Mom lifts the coffee pot and pours some into a mug. The steam rises into the air. She blows it away and sips. "Have you started unpacking?" "Sort of." I stir the cereal around. "Amelia, try to get it done today." She leans her hip into the counter. "I will, I will." "Oh and make sure you take the empty boxes up to the attic. We could probably use them later." Groan. She tilts the mug to drink the remainder of coffee. "Ok I have to go get dressed." She places the mug in one side of the sink and rubs my shoulder as she passes by. "Get dressed? Where are you going?" "I met some other moms." She continues to talk while she walks upstairs. "To welcome me they're going to take me to a few boutiques and then have lunch. Isn't that sweet?" Great, she gets to go out today, and I have to stay home and unpack. Its Saturday, I want to go out too. I don't know who I would go out with, but still. I put my lips around the rim of the bowl and sip the remaining milk. I place it in the sink and drag one of the boxes labeled-- *Lia's Stuff* upstairs to my room. I guess I better get started.

☽

Four hours, thirty-two minutes, six seconds, and a slight backache later I'm unpacking the last thing. A tall, thin, white floor lamp--I plug it in, click it on and a glow illuminates throughout my room. Done. I look at the empty boxes surrounding me. My tiredness decides for me that I'll take them up to the attic tomorrow. I grab a towel and my robe. I definitely need a shower. I turn on the light and quickly glance in the mirror. Something horrible is reflected. I jump back, crashing into the towel rack. Was that… a wolf? I grimace, rubbing the small of my back. I pull myself up using the sink. I slowly creep up looking into the mirror. First I see my eyes, then my nose, then my lips. I touch my face and poke it as I lean closer to the mirror. Okay, its official, I'm crazy. I try to shake the image. I turn on the shower, disrobe, and step in. It feels good and warm. I close my eyes, leaning my head back, letting the water jump all over my face. Three minutes of shower time was all I got when the doorbell sounded. Sigh. I step out, grab a towel, and pull my robe off the hook. I put it on as I'm practically slipping down the steps. The bell sounds again. I reach the front door and pull it open, irritated. He's standing there--in relaxed fit jeans and a black long sleeved t-shirt. His cologne lightly scents the air. I'm not irritated anymore. "Hey" he smiles. "I'm sorry I didn't mean to just drop by." He looks down at the trickling of water coming down my legs. Crap it looks like I'm peeing on myself. This couldn't get any more embarrassing. "Oh no its fine" I wipe my legs down with the towel. "I was in the shower when I heard the doorbell. "Sorry about that. I just was wondering if maybe you and I could go somewhere." "Where?" I ask, trying to disguise my excitement. "I don't know somewhere, I haven't decided." He smiles again pushing his hands in his pockets. "I, um, ok, give me like five minutes." He agrees and walks into the entry way. "Just make yourself comfortable." I yell while running up the stairs. When I open my door Jojo's lying on the rug in the same position she was in when I went to take my shower. I step over her, walk into my closet, and pull out a pair of khaki pants. I start looking for a top. Wow, I do have a lot of tank tops. I find a thin white sweater that hangs low on one side exposing my shoulder. Jojo lifts her head slowly as she watches me knock into the floor lamp trying to quickly pull the sweater on and oil n brush through my hair quickly. I look in my floor length mirror. Not bad for five minutes. I rush downstairs, this hurriedness catches Jojo's attention and she runs behind me. "I'm ready." I announce, slyly trying to catch my breath. He gets up. Jojo's rests next to my feet. He walks towards me, Jojo lifts up slowly, her snarl becoming louder. "Jojo, stop that." She snaps her bark. She looks so vicious and he surprisingly seems calm. "Jojo, stop that, now!" I demand. I pull her by her collar into a nearby bedroom and close the door. "I'm sorry--she never ever acted like that before. That's why my dad and I adopted her in the first place-- we could tell she was a good, easy going dog." "It's okay, maybe there's just something about me she doesn't like." He softly shrugs his shoulders. "Ready?" He opens the door and lets me walk before him. "Oh wait I have to lock the door." As I turn to, he softly grabs my arm, pulling me into a body pressing hug. "There's no need to lock doors in the Falls." He looks deeply into my eyes. I look back. His eyes are so black and glossy I can clearly see my reflection. I smile. "But I should, just to be sure." "Well at least let me lock it for you." He's still chivalrous and cute. I agree and give him the key. He walks to the front door and turns back, walking towards his car seconds later. He opens the door for me and closes it after I slide all the way in. Zev starts the rumbling engine. "So have you decided where we're going?" I pull my seatbelt on. "Yeah I have." He puts the car in gear and takes off. It's a quiet drive, but not awkward, just comfortable. I feel Zev slide his hand on my thigh and lace our fingers together. He keeps his concentration on the winding road. His lips form a slight smile. I smile too. I can feel the blood quickly pumping through my veins. There goes my heart again. I wonder if he can hear it, its beating so hard. Although I'm enjoying the connection between us I can't help but notice that the road seems endless. He finally slows down and veers off to the right stopping short of the edge of a grassy hill. I don't really want to get out the car. I don't see any signs that this place is somewhere I want to be. Where are we anyways? He opens my door and extends his hand, I take it. The hill is steep so he crawls down first and grabs my waist to give me support. My body brushes against his as he pulls me down, his enigmatic eyes pull me in again. "Come on" he whispers without breaking his stare.

Chapter 6

"Where are we?" I follow closely behind him down the soft dirt road. He keeps walking without giving an answer. Damp overgrown grass swipes against my pants leaving wet marks and low-hanging branches roughly brush against my face. We stop at a small cabin. It's old and sagging, wood planks are missing from the roof, and the windows look like they've been shattered. He opens the door and invites me in. I step in, slowly looking around at the inside. It's not much better than the outside. A fire is already roaring. A large blanket is laid across the floor adorned with plush pillows. Two stemmed glasses stand next to a small tray of chocolate covered strawberries and small rose petals are scattered everywhere. Despite the shabbiness of the cabin, it's a perfect cover for a romance novel. "Sit down." He smiles softly. I do, leaning into the pillows for comfort. I take a strawberry and bite into its sweet goodness. He walks into the kitchen area, I hear a pop, and he comes back holding a bottle. "Is that wine?" I tease. "No, of course not, it's sparkling cider." He grins and pours some into both of our glasses. I taste it. It's definitely cider. He doesn't drink from his. Instead he places it down and moves closer to me. "I know that it's only been two days that we've known each other but I like you, Lia." His eyes flicker. "I, um, like you too Zev." I'm so embarrassed. "It was something I sensed about you the first time I saw you." He leans closer. "Oh, you did?" I feel my throat getting dry. Why am I so nervous? I've had a guy this close to me before-- of course he wasn't this cute. He softly places his finger under my chin and tilts it up. His lips look softer the closer he gets. I'm frozen. He leans in-- his full lips are inches away from mine. I close my eyes and slightly purse my lips together waiting for the kiss, when it happens. Something crashes into the side of the cabin. The impact hits so hard the cabin's structure rumbles and a thin sheet of dust falls from the ceiling. We both jump to our feet. "What was that?!" I'm breathing heavy. He presses his index finger over his lips to quiet me and walks to the window. "I don't know. I don't see anything." He turns and tries to reassure me. "It was probably nothing." Noting my obvious fear, Zev rubs the sides of my arms and kisses my cheek. "Come on, I'll take you home." He starts picking up the wine glasses. I walk towards the door and it slams opens before I could reach for the handle. I scream while this animal grabs me by my leg and begins to drag me. My head slams against the dusty wooden floor and it instantly dazes me. Seconds later I wake from my daze, my stomach and chest is being scraped against the sticks, grass, and dirt. I'm reaching and screaming for Zev, who's standing in the doorway, watching me get dragged. He starts to grow smaller the further away I get. "Zev!" I cry again, my trembled screams quiet when my throat hits against a dirt-covered rock. I look up a last time. I can see him shake his head and drop the glasses. He runs, so fast, it's almost unreal. He growls as he pulls my leg out of the grip of my captor and throws his keys on the ground. "Go!" he rumbles his demand, his eyes completely golden. I'm lying on my back, stunned, I feel like my body is glued to the ground. I stare at him and what he's fighting…I think it's a… wolf? "Go!" he snarls. I get up, snatch the keys, and run for what seems like forever. I see his creamy car shining under the moonlight. I pull my body up the steep hill using upper body strength I didn't even know I had. I scramble to the car and lean against it, fumbling around in the darkness trying to unlock the door. I slide into the large front seat. Something large and hairy hurls itself at me just as soon as I close the door. I scream, tightly closing my eyes, wrapping my arms around my head. I thought I was cured of my asthma when I was ten, apparently not. The wheezing begins and hot tears drop onto my thighs; calm down, Lia. Calm down. I slowly lift my head up and look out the window. Remnants of fur are stuck to it. I stare at the traces of hair until a soft wind blows them off the window. I put the key in the ignition and back up quickly, racing to get home.

Chapter 7

I'm zooming on a twisted, dark road with no headlights. I'm so scared I can't think straight. My hands shake as I try to get a grip on the slick steering wheel. I continue driving into darkness. I fumble around the darkened panel searching for a button or switch, anything to trigger the headlights. I can feel the car pulling into the other side of the lane. My fingers twist around a knob. I turn it. An oncoming car is illuminated and the driver sounds their horn. I swerve, just missing a tree. The bright lights cut through the dark allowing me to see the road all the way until I reach a familiar street. I pull into the long driveway. I see my mom's old Benz parked in its usual spot. I cut off the lights and park Zev's Mustang right behind it. I open the door and fall out of the seat. My face hits the dirt and suddenly, my brain feels like it's been in a blender. I can't concentrate. What's happening? I drag myself across the ground. I use the railing of the steps to pull myself up. I yank my house key out of my pants pocket. I pull it out and struggle to unlock the door. I stagger into the entryway and make my way to the staircase, stumbling up each step. My room is black, except for the streams of moonlight gleaming through the window. I collapse onto my bed, holding both my house key and Zev's car keys. The last thing I hear is a distant wolf's howl.

☽

I feel patters on my chest. "Zev?" I softly mumble. "No, I'm not Zev." My mom's voice rings clear. "Get up. Where were you last night?" she sits on the edge of my bed, pulling only my house key out of my hand and placing it on the side table. I look at my hand, I remember two keys. "I was worried Amelia. You could have left a note, called my cell, anything." Her voice is full of concern. She looks at me and grabs my chin. "I know your seventeen and you have a little boyfriend now but that doesn't make you an adult and it certainly doesn't mean you can just leave without telling me." She softly pats my cheek. "And look at the mess you left with these boxes. I thought I asked you to put them in the attic." She stands and puts her hands on her hips. I can't focus enough to say anything to my mom. All I feel is hot and sweaty. Exasperated, she rubs my forehead. "Are you okay?" "Yeah" I squeeze out. "Amelia, don't start acting wild, okay? I know being a teenager is exciting and going to parties and getting drunk seems fun, at the time, but then look at the side effects you wake up with. Next time you and Zev party all night, you better let me know. Although I don't think there will be a next time for awhile seeing as your grounded for the next month or two." She smiles quickly, her blue eyes glisten. "I'm going to be downstairs. In a couple hours I'll come wake you up to clean up these boxes. Oh, and next time you decide to leave, at least lock the door, anybody could have gotten in here." I did lock the door. I mean Zev was supposed to lock it for me. She exits, closing my door. I can hear the steps creak as she makes her way downstairs. Groan. I wipe more sweat from my forehead. What happened last night? I pull the covers back and look down at my body-- it's in my flowery pajama pants and oversized t-shirt. I look at my nails, they are caked with dirt. Images flash quickly of me clawing my nails into the dirt. I press my hands against my forehead. A gush of wind chills me. I get up quickly and notice the open window. I rush over to close it and look down onto the front yard. Deep tire tracks are behind my mom's car that form a "U" like the driver did a quick turn before taking off. I lock the window and take a breath. I look down and see dried, muddy footprints make tracks to my bed, and then they stop. I pull myself backwards onto the bed and lay back down, pulling my knees towards my chest. What happened? I keep asking, hoping someone can give me answer. I must have fallen asleep because when my mom bursts through the door, it startles me awake. My eyes are open at their widest staring at her. "Rise and shine! Its noon and it's time for you to get started with your chores." "Chores?" I lie back down and pull the covers over my head. "Since when do I have chores?" I roll my eyes under the blanket. "Since," she whips the blankets back "you decided to be so irresponsible yesterday." She smacks my butt. "Come on, up, up, up." "Mom!" I rub where she slapped it tender. "Shower, brush your teeth, run in place, do whatever you need to do to get out of bed. See you downstairs in ten minutes." She closes the door and leaves me cold, tired, and with a butt-ache. I pull myself to sit straight up. Groggily, I grab my robe and head for the shower. I flip the switch and look into the mirror and this time it's only me in my reflection. Thank God. I take off my pajamas and throw them in the clothes hamper. I step into the steaming shower and close my eyes, first letting the water trickle over me. I pour shampoo in my hands and start to massage it through my hair. Wet sticks and leaves untangle themselves and fall to the drain. I grab the soap and rub it against my stomach and I flinch and gasp; the sting is unbearable. I look down and small streams of blood are making their way from the cuts in my stomach, down my legs, and into the shower drain. I know this had something to do with last night. All I can remember was that I was with…Zev and I…I was struggling. He wouldn't hurt me, would he? Ten minutes later, I'm out of the shower, hair pulled back, wearing a tank top and sweatpants ready to do these chores and get them over with. My mom is trying to connect our TV to the DVD player. She looks at me in frustration. "Since there is no cable right now, I figured I could at least get the DVD player hooked up and watch something." "Let me try." I suggest. I walk towards the TV and pick up a pink and white ball in the walkway-- Jojo's favorite ball. "Jojo come here girl, Jojo..." I whistle. She doesn't come. I remember I put her in an extra bedroom yesterday after her vicious dog routine. Definitely time to free her from her temporary confinement. "Hold on mom, I'm going to let Jojo out." "Sure." Her hands are tangled in wires. This extra bedroom is empty and large so Jojo shouldn't have gone too stir crazy. I hope. "Hey, girl" I say as I open the door to an empty room. There's no retriever running to me and practically knocking me down, trying to lick my cheeks."Jojo?" I walk to the center of the room. "Jojo?!" Worriedly, I run to the living room. "Mom, Jojo's gone!" She looks up from her tangled mess. "What?" "Jojo is gone. I put her in that room yesterday." I point to the bedroom I just came out of. My mom looks confused. "Well, yesterday when I came home that door was open." I continue to listen to her. "Which I thought was strange because we never leave doors open because Jojo always gets into things and sometimes uses the bathroom where she's not supposed to." My mom begins to fumble with the twisted wires again. I don't even think I'm listening now. I'm thinking about Jojo, Zev, and whatever else happened yesterday. "Don't worry I'm sure Jojo's fine. She just got out. She may even be close by." Mom tries to reassure me. I open the front door and call her name. No answer. I try again. No answer. Maybe if I whistle. After three failed attempts my mom calls to me from the living room. "Amelia, close the door you're letting a draft in, I'm sure Jojo is fine. Tomorrow you and I will go out to look for her." She stands up and faces me. Sigh. She holds up the wiry mess. "Can I have some help?" I connect the DVD player for my mom. Afterwards, she hurriedly chooses a movie and lies on the couch wrapped in a thick blanket. She has a bowl of salted chips rested on her lap and a glass of wine on the coffee table. She smiles at me. "Hey, enjoy your chores?" she teases. I turn and start doing my chore of cleaning the kitchen. It takes me an hour and a half to realize that this kitchen needs to be renovated-- it's old, some tiles on the counter top and floor are seriously chipped, and there's more mildew than a kitchen could have. There's only so much cleaning that can be done in this situation. I throw the sopping sponge in the trash. It just barely balances on top of the overflowing heap of garbage. I guess I'll have to empty it. I yank the garbage bag out of the trash can. It has to weigh over ten pounds. We need to empty the trash more often. I start dragging it against the floor. I pass the living room. My mom has drifted off to sleep and the credits begin to ascend up a black screen. I keep dragging. I'm walking backwards, my butt in the air. I stop to open the door and return to my trash-pulling position. The trash can is rolled against the side of the house. I keep dragging through the dirt and foliage. I lift the large top and it flaps back. Flies rise from the bottom to their freedom along with a moldy smell. I turn my face away while trying to lift the bag. My skinny arms certainly weren't made for this type of work. I finally got the bag lifted in the air when something touches my back. I scream. The bag crashes to the ground, most of the garbage spilling out. "I'm sorry." He bends down to gather the trash, throwing it in the can. My hand clutches my chest and I try to slow my breathing. "Do you like coming over to people's house unannounced?" I snap. I pull the top back down and start walking towards my front door. "Lia, wait, please." He asks, but I don't listen. "Please wait." As soon as I reach the steps, I stop. He softly grabs my arm and turns me to face him. "Was that all I was to you?" "What are you talking about?" "You take me to that crappy cabin, drug me with cider, do whatever else you did to me and then take off?!" I say pointing to the tire track impressions. "How could you do that to me?" "No, Lia I didn't do anything, I swear. It's not what you're thinking, okay." He grabs my hand, I pull it away. "Lia, listen there are things you don't understand yet, things about me…and you." His eyes are sympathetic. "I don't want to lie to you, but I don't know how to tell you the truth." He looks down. I shake my head. "And what about locking my door? You lied to me then. You told me you locked it!" I push him in his chest. "And now Jojo's gone!"My hands pounds against his chest, he grabs them, yanks me towards him and presses his lips against mine. I close my eyes and feel my body relax as he massages his lips with mine. He cups one side my face with a firm hand and runs the tip of his fingers from my roots all the way through my hair, resting his other hand on my back. I pull away and stare at him. "Lia, I swear you have the wrong idea about last night…" "Well I have a right idea at the moment, stay away from me." I run into the house and slam the door. My mom pops up from her sleep. "What happened, Lia, are you okay?" I rush upstairs, burning with anger. "I'm fine." I hurry to my room and throw myself on the bed .I'm so angry. I can't believe Zev would do that to me and then lie to my face about it. I hate him. I hate him! My lips are tingling. I close my eyes and see his usually chiseled brown face softened by sadness; his tearful eyes burning into mine. He makes it so hard to hate him.

Chapter 8

Two hours later I try to rise up enough from my love-hate dilemma to decide what to do about Jojo. Should I post missing dog signs, maybe offer a reward? I sit at my desk and click on the lamp, with note paper and a marker I write-- *Missing Dog- light tan retriever. If you find her please call* 877-5555. I haven't seen any dogs around here, so Jojo should be easy to spot if she is found, hopefully. I write up ten of these and stack them neatly. I pull on my boots, grab the stack of papers and make my way downstairs. My mom is in the kitchen tasting the sauce she's cooking for the noodles. She turns slightly. "Hey, I cooked your favorite." I place my signs on the counter and go to the hall closet searching for my rain coat. I pull it on and button it up. "Where are you going?" she lifts her eyebrow and reaches for one of the signs, she reads it. "I'm going to post these signs and look for Jojo." "No you're not. Do you see that storm out there?" The rain is falling in heavy layers and the thunder makes a jagged line in the dark navy sky as if to emphasize what she said. "Mom, I'm going, Jojo could be hurt or something and I'm not going to let her be out there in this weather." I pick up the paper stack and head towards the front door. "Amelia Joan Brewer, get back here right now! You're my daughter and you will listen to me. I'm not letting you go out in weather like this to search for Jojo." She's serious now. Her blue eyes grow intense and her lips tighten. I slam the papers down on the countertop, quickly unbutton my jacket, throw it across the back of the chair, and dart upstairs. "This is so unfair." I yell before slamming my door. I anxiously pace across my room. I glance at my clock radio- 6:42, it reads in fluorescent green numbers. My face reddens with anger. She never liked Jojo anyways! She probably wouldn't even care if Jojo died out there! It was me and dad's dog, not hers! Now Jojo's gone, I feel like I have no one. I fall face first on my bed, tears wetting my pillow. "Daddy, I miss you!" I cry. Soft knocks sound from outside my door. "Go away." "Amelia." my mom opens the door. "Calm down, please." A flood of emotions escapes. "It's your fault he's gone. Your fault!" I sit up facing my mother, my face stained with tears. "You made him go get your stupid bottle of wine, like you couldn't go one damn dinner without a glass of it!" Her blue eyes become watery. "And we waited and waited and he never came back. And hours later a cop comes to our door and tells us he was in a car accident." I start breathing quickly. "I didn't even get to say goodbye." I drop my forehead in my palms and cry. She begins to cry too. "I…miss your father just as much you do, Amelia." "Call me Lia! I hate Amelia!" She intensely stares, tears slowly rolling down her reddened cheeks. "I hate being here…with you." My voice drops along with my eyes. I'm staring at my fuzzy rug where Jojo used to lazily lay. She swallows and softly massages her throat. I pull my legs up to my chest and keep my stare at the rug. "Well, if that's how you feel…we'll have to change that. You're my daughter and I don't want you to be unhappy." She leaves. Now I feel even more horrible and alone. I lay down on my side in a room of silence. A soft buzz breaks the quiet. I grab my cell phone and read the screen-- *New message*. I wipe my eyes so I can read the message clearly. *Do you know why this place is called Wolf Falls?*

A message sent from Zev. I don't know why it's called Wolf Falls. My dad would never tell me completely. He would only answer "there's a lot wolves." And when I asked him why he would want to move back to a place full of wolves, he looked away and continued whatever he was doing. He never gave me a full answer and at this point I could care less. I erase the message and put my phone back on the table. I lie on my stomach and close my eyes. Drops of rain begin to patter against my window. I squeeze my pillow over my head. I just want to go away…especially from here.

Chapter 9

I wake up to knocking. Ugh. My mom opens the door and starts carrying a suitcase out, a purple one that I recognize…its mine. I tumble out of bed and quickly follow her downstairs. "Where are you going with my suitcase?" "I'm not going anywhere. You are." She stands it by the front door next to my small duffel bag. "You should get dressed. We're leaving in twenty minutes." "Leaving to where?!" I cross my arms over my chest. "Apparently you don't want to be here with me right now and I think some time away from each other will do us both good. I called Aunt Kerry and she's glad to have you over." "So you're throwing me out to live with your sister." "It's only for a week or two, Amelia." She sighs. I recoil when she calls me that. No use in arguing, at least I'll be away from here. Upstairs, I take almost an hour to get ready. Why rush? "Amelia." I hear my mom call me. "We were supposed to have left awhile ago. It's getting late." she shouts. "I'm coming." I zip up my hoodie as I amble down the stairs. I swoop up my duffel bag, resting the strap on my shoulder and roll the suitcase to the car. I throw my bags in the backseat and slam the door. I get in the front seat, slamming the door again. "Okay, enough with the door slamming." She orders. As soon as the drive starts I pull my MP3 player out of my pocket, press the buds into my ears, and scroll to a fast-paced song. It's a three hour ride to Aunt Kerry's house and I don't plan on talking or listening. I turn the volume up and let the music drown out any external noises. The first half hour of the drive I'm still pissed at this whole situation but at least I'm getting out of the Falls. I sink my back into the seat. This trip might not be such a bad idea.

☽

I've been staring out the window for an hour now. Trees are the only thing to look at. How scenic. I decide to stare at the roof of the car, not a bad alternative. My stomach growls quietly. I'm so hungry. I didn't get to eat any of my mom's spaghetti last night and I haven't gotten a chance to eat anything since then. My mom taps on my shoulder. I pull one of my buds out. "Yeah?" "Are you hungry?" I guess my stomach didn't growl as quietly as I thought. I shrug. "I guess." But of course on this tree infested road there isn't anywhere to stop. A half hour more of driving and a large sign that reads half a mile with a picture of a plate and fork comes into view. "Well I guess it's half a mile till we eat." She suggests. I push my bud back in my ear and resume the current song. Half a mile later my mom parks in the space directly in front of the entrance of Sid's Diner. I really don't want to go in. The whole atmosphere doesn't seem too inviting. Of course my mom doesn't feel the same way. "Come on." She slides out of the car grabbing her purse. I hesitate. She bends down, poking her head inside the car. "Come on. I thought you were hungry." "I am." Ugh. I don't want to eat here. I slowly open the door and get out. She opens the glass door for me and a petite bell clinks against it. The waitress, who is at a booth, taking an order, looks up from her notepad and maintains her stare. Her eyes disgustingly look me up and down. My mom pulls me to a booth in the back and slides in. "Well this place is charming." She softly smiles looking at her surroundings. "Sure, if dirty and a little smelly is your definition for charming." The long fluorescent bulb buzzes above our heads. The table has pieces of dried food stuck to it which prevents me from leaning on it. Gross. My mom slides a small menu card over to me. I don't know if it's safe to eat here. But my stomach keeps sounding reminders that I need to eat something. I choose a cheeseburger with fries. That waitress comes to our table, reluctantly I'm sure. She looks a lot older up close. Her overly made–upped face doesn't cover her wrinkles as well as she thinks it does. Her long reddish braid is slung over her shoulder. She rudely pops her gum and lifts her notepad out her apron. She smiles at my mom. "What can I get for you?" "I think I'll have the meatloaf and mashed potatoes." The waitress, whose nametag reads Shelby, quickly scribbles down the order and turns to me. Her expression turns grim. She stares down at me, slowly blinking while she pops her bright blue chewing gum. "I guess it's my turn." I lift my eyebrow. "Hmmm…" I pretend like I'm reading the menu. I tap my chin with my finger. She shifts her weight to her fleshy hip and crosses her arms over her chest. "Oh um I'll have…no, never mind, I don't want that." She blows a bubble and snaps it in her mouth, letting out a heavy sigh. "Okay I'll have a cheesebu-" Shelby quickly interjects. "We're all out of meat." "Well how are they going to make my mom's meatloaf?" I look up to her waiting for an answer. She just stares. "Maybe you should order something else." My mom suggests looking at the menu. "What about a grilled cheese, Amelia?" "We were running low on cheese. I'm not sure if there's any left." My mom looks up at that. Shelby quickly smiles. "But I'll check with the cook to see if there's any left." She scribbles on her bent notepad again and shuffles away. I look around the hole-in-the-wall eatery-- totally crummy. There are five booths and seven stools lining the counter. A couple cheaply framed pictures sloppily hang on 1970's wallpaper and a TV, that looks like it hasn't worked in a while, is stationed in an upper corner of a wall. There's a large open window so you can see the cook. I watch him as he takes the order from Shelby, she impolitely points to me, and he looks up with an intense stare. He wipes the sweat off his forehead and wipes his nose with back of his hand. His greasy, chubby face stares while Shelby continues to talk and point. Nervously, I pull my hair to my side and begin to play with the edges. "You need a trim." My mom notes, staring at the ends of my hair. "I don't know what it is but since you were a little girl no matter how much I trimmed and cut your hair it'd be grown back in about two days." She recalls, softly wiping her fork with a napkin. "Your hair is just like your dad's, he would get haircuts and his hair would be grown back the next day. He was so hairy." She laughs at her thought. I push my hair behind my back and look out the window at the parking lot. Noticing I'm not in the mood to reminisce she decides to stop talking. It remains quiet at our booth until Mom begins to softly drum her fingers on the table. "It sure is taking awhile to make our food." She pushes her sleeve back to look at her small-faced silver watch. I notice the twenty minute lapse too, but I'm not in a rush to eat food from here. "It's not like there's a crowd of people. I wish they would hurry, we really need to get back on the road." As if to grant her wish, Shelby walks to our table balancing two plates. "For you." She softly sits the plate down in front of my mom. She turns to me and is just short of throwing my plate into my lap. "Enjoy." She directs that only to my mom. My mom's plate is divided between a large helping of mashed potatoes covered in steaming gravy and large slice of well-cooked meatloaf. "It looks good." My mom cuts a piece of meatloaf with her fork and begins eating. I look down at my plate-- a near-burnt half of a grilled cheese sandwich and four French fries. "How's your food?" she looks up from her plate. I shrug. She pulls my plate closer. "Amelia I'm going to order you something else that looks horrible." She tries to get the waitress' attention. "No, it's fine mom, really."

"Are you sure? It doesn't even look appetizing." A concerned look takes over her face. "At least have some of mine. She begins to scrape some mashed potatoes from her plate. I stop her. "No, I'm ok. Thanks." I pull the plate back and eat a fry. It's cold. I drown the other three fries in ketchup and force them down. I eat a bite of my grilled cheese and put it back. Burnt isn't a favorite taste of mine. My mom finishes her deluxe meal shortly before the fifteen minute mark. Shelby promptly places a receipt on the table. Mom reads it, pulls a twenty dollar bill out her purse and rests it on top of the receipt. I'd rather eat the bottom of my shoe than pay for the food here. She gets up. "I'll be right back. I'm going to the restroom." "Okay" I pull my cell phone out of my pocket and see that I have four text messages and two missed calls, all from Zev. My heart flutters at the sight of his name but quickly hardens when I think about what he did or what I think he did. I get frustrated with myself just thinking about that night. So I try not to. I delete the messages without reading them and slide my phone back in my hoodie's pocket. I don't want to think about Zev or the Falls or his rude friends, especially Aja. The non-stop buzzing of the overhead lights, the hideous décor, and the rude waitress is all beginning to annoy the crap out of me. I decide to go wait in the car. I slide out of the booth. When I turn from grabbing my mom's purse a seething look is burning into me. This time it's not from the waitress or the cook, but from a burly guy with no hair except for a short braid grown from his chin. His worn leather jacket is just barely fitting around his large arms and even larger waist. Since he obviously can't close his jacket, it's revealing a holster that's strapped to his waist. A sliver gun handle is exposed. I stare at it. I've seen guns before but not so stainless steel and shiny, I would probably be able to see my reflection if I got closer to it. He squints at me and turns away. The back of his jacket has a large grotesque stitching of a wolf being shot to death. Above the stitching are curved silver words-- The Seekers. I notice that there are two more men wearing the same jacket staring at me with the same disgust. It seems everyone here feels that way towards me considering that the cook and the waitress haven't given their nasty looks a rest since I walked in. Whatever. I know what it is. It's because I'm half black and half white, mixed, biracial, whatever you want to call it. Deal with it. I have. Well I'm trying to. I didn't even notice my mom come out of the restroom. "Amelia, did you need to use the bathroom?" she asks. I realize I'm standing stationary next to the booth. "No, no, I was getting ready to go wait in the car." I give mom her purse. "Oh, well now you don't have to wait." My mom walks past those men. They shoot her a smile and quickly change to a murderous expression when I approach. I feel scared and panicky. Something comes over me and I feel like I'm going to implode. My body begins to burn all over. I've never felt anything like this. My eyes begin to sting. I try to shake this feeling. In the mirror's reflection by the entryway I watch my eyes turn to almost a clear golden brown-- so piercing and vivid. Burly sees my eyes, infuriated he jumps up from the stool. Another guy, shorter and bald also, grabs his arms and pulls him down. Burly sneers. "I hate her kind." I hear horn honks. "Amelia?! Come on." I rush outside and get in the car quickly, slamming the door. I pull myself up to look in the review mirror and my eyes are back to brown. I examine my eyes and pull the skin under them down. I blink hard and open my eyes again, no change. "What were you doing?" she turns the engine over. "Uh, nothing" I pull myself down in the seat. "Are you alright?" she touches my arm sleeve and pulls away quickly. "You're burning up. I can feel it through your sleeve." She starts touching my forehead and my cheeks. "It feels like you're on fire." "I'm fine mom, please." I push her hand away. She sighs. "Maybe we should go home and I can find you a doctor." "No, I said I'm fine. I'm just warm, I *am* wearing a hoodie." "Fine, Amelia." She digs in her bag and pulls out a clear tube full of pink liquid. While my mom applies her lip gloss the Seekers exit the restaurant-- their stainless steel guns shining against their waist. They stare at me as they straddle their motorcycles. "Can we just get out of here?" She purses her lips and evens out the lip gloss with the tip of her finger. "Alright, we're going, we're going." She places the tube back in her bag and drives out of the parking lot onto a darkened highway, the Seekers remaining far in the distance.

Chapter 10

About two hours later we're pulling into a roundabout drive way surrounded by grassiness and petite flowers that landscapes the entrance to a large brick house with deep red double doors-- my Aunt's house. I'm not really that close to my aunt. We get along and stuff but as far as let's bake cookies together and tell each other secrets, um I don't think so. But she's cool...for an aunt. My mom told me she was living comfortably but this looks a little more than comfortable. I wonder who affords this. I'm guessing her husband, what's his name? It's right on the tip of my tongue. Anyways, I don't know much about him. The little that I do know is that he is some type of business man, sounds boring. Aunt Kerry told my mom he's always away, traveling for his company, so most of the time it's just her and Abby, my cousin. Ugh, this should be fun. I'm surprised that I'm even going to stay here. Mom and Aunt Kerry had a big fight before my aunt's wedding and never really talked much after that. It was a little over a year ago in New York, in our old apartment. They were yelling at each other at the top of their lungs. My mom didn't agree with her marrying him because he is almost twenty years older than my twenty-four year old aunt. Because of that fact Mom decided to voice her thoughts, loudly, declaring that she refused to be in Aunt Kerry's wedding or even come if she married Rick, yeah that's his name. A week later the wedding went on-- for once my mom didn't get her way. "Well, we're here. Are you going to get out or just stare?" My mom pulls the key out of the ignition. I begin pulling my suitcase out of the backseat while slinging my duffel bag over my shoulder. Mom's in front of me running her fingers through her hair, puffing her chest out, and softly puckering her lips. That's her "I'm hot" look. So embarrasing. When we reach the doorstep, she checks her reflection in the bolted stainless steel sign next to the door that has *The Hurston's* fancily stamped into it. She presses her finger against a glowing button, a chime sounds. Aunt Kerry opens the door-- she's a reflection of my mother-- blonde hair, pale skin, high cheekbones and small eyes. Only difference is Aunt Kerry's eyes are brown. She's dressed in a thick white turtleneck that stops mid her thigh and black leggings. "I thought something happened to you two." She invites us in. My mom steps in and looks around the foyer, I walk behind her. A large staircase winds upward and a small chair, table, and mirror are positioned against the adjacent wall. "We're late because Amelia took forever to get dressed and then we stopped to get something to eat." "I could have cooked." She points to herself. My mom snorts softly. "Would that be ramen noodles or a delicious frozen burrito?" Aunt Kerry stares at my mother, her lips growing thin as her anger heightens. That looks familiar. I softly place my duffel bag on the wood floor. "Oh, let me take you to where you'll be staying." She starts walking upstairs, I follow and so does my mother. She stops at the first door across from the landing. She opens the door, flips the switch, and the ceiling light illuminates a spacious, obvious guest room. The room has minimal amount of furniture-- a bed, a TV, and two floor lamps. I place my things next to the bed and we all walk back downstairs and go into the living room. Aunt Kerry leans against a table, I sit on the suede sofa and Mom sits across from me in the matching chair, looking at her finger nails. I'm waiting for the awkwardness to go away. I don't think it will. Aunt Kerry walks over to the play pen and picks up Abby. Her two blonde wispy ponytails are secured in place with pink bows. She's dressed in pink pants and a white frilly t-shirt. Mom's eyes lighten up. "Kerry she's adorable." Abby begins to reach for my mom. "You want to go to Aunt Joan?" Aunt Kerry coos as she hands Abby over. Mom twirls a finger around one of Abby's ponytail. "You are so cute, yes you are." Abby gives a one-tooth smile as my mom kisses her plump cheek. "How old is she Kerry?" "She'll be one in a month." "I wish I could have made it to the baby shower." My mom looks at Aunt Kerry. "Yeah, well you could have come if you weren't being so…immature about the wedding." Ignoring that comment my mom gets up and carries Abby over to me. Great, like I really want slobber all over me. "This is your cousin, Amelia." Mom tells Abby as she brings her closer to me. Abby looks at me and begins to cry. Not just shedding a few tears, she's kicking and screaming her face turning beat red. Aunt Kerry reaches for Abby and pulls her to her chest, softly rubbing her back. "What's wrong Abby?" she asks softly. "She's probably just cranky." Aunt Kerry smiles nervously. I just look. "I should probably put her down for bedtime." Aunt Kerry comes back after a few minutes. "I think she was tired. As soon as I lied her down she went to sleep." She reasons. Mom rises from the plush oversized chair, "I'm going to go ahead and leave now. It's already after 8:00, and I don't want to get home too late." Aunt Kerry agrees, so do I, and we all say our goodbyes. Well my goodbye was a wave as I walk upstairs to the guest room, but a goodbye none the less. I pull the floral comforter up to my chin as I turn on my side. "Amelia?" Aunt Kerry knocks on the door. "Come in." She flips the lights on and smiles. "Are you already in bed?" "Yeah, four hours was a long drive." She nods. "I can imagine." Aunt Kerry stands in the doorway and I pull the covers up to just below my eyes.

She notices my obvious desire to sleep. “Well I guess I’ll let you sleep, sweet dreams.” She turns the light out and gently closes the door.

Chapter 11

I sit up again and look around the darkened room. I heard it again, that noise I've been hearing for the last three hours. It's making it difficult to sleep. It sounds like its coming from the attic. I look up at the ceiling. Maybe I should go wake up Aunt Kerry and ask her what it is. Although, I could be overreacting it's probably a rat or something. I lie back down on the bed, listening to the scratching, probably a very large rat. With the money Aunt Kerry and her husband obviously have they could at least hire an exterminator. I convince myself it's only a rodent and press my eyes shut until I fall asleep. And I do, but it sounds again, waking me up. Okay that's it I'm going to wake her up. I quickly get up, tripping out of the elevated bed. Crap. I grab my ankle. I manage to hobble out of the room only to be frightened. I scream, she screams. "Amelia, it's just me." She grabs my shoulders. "Aunt Kerry!" "Yes!" Even in the dark she can see the frightened look on my face. "Are you alright?" "I, um, I was just…" she waits for an answer. "Were you trying to find the bathroom? It occurred to me that I never showed you where it was." "Yeah, I was looking for it." "Come on" she leads me to a small bathroom down the hall. "Aunt Kerry" I hesitate "have you been hearing noises?" She turns to face me. "No, why have you?" "I have, but it's probably just animals or something." "There *are* a lot of cats around here." She clicks the light on for the restroom and I notice she's holding a flat colorful book. "*Rabbit's Exciting Adventures*, were you reading that?" I point to the book. She laughs. "Oh no, this is Abby's favorite book. She woke up shortly after you went to sleep. I was reading to her and fell asleep in the rocking chair." "Oh."I stand in the bathroom doorway, not really wanting to go back to the room. "Do you think you can find your way back?" She jokes. I smile weakly "yeah". The bathroom is small and clean, very clean. There's just a sink and a toilet. Everything is sterile white-- the tiles, the toilet, the mirror, the cabinetry, and the hand towels neatly hanging from a white towel rack. Way too much white. I look at my face in the mirror, puffy eyes stares back. I splash my face with water, open my eyes and in the mirror's reflection I see something at the window. I quickly turn to look and he's not there…Zev. Okay now I'm hallucinating. I start wetting my face with water until its dripping. I take a deep breath and look at the window again; just a shining half-moon in a black, star-scattered sky. I roll my eyes at my thought of Zev. Why am I even thinking about him? I have better things to think about, I persuade myself. I turn out the light and limp back to my room. Don't think about him at all, just go to sleep. Just go to sleep.

☽

Abby's cries wake me up. My cell phone displays 7:54 a.m. I sit up and bend my left ankle back and forth until it doesn't feel so stressed. I get up slowly and balance. I walk down the steps shifting most of my weight onto my right foot. Abby's in her highchair, turning her face away from the orange strained food on the spoon Aunt Kerry's holding in the air. "Good morning, Amelia. Did Abby wake you up?" "No." I lie. Of course she did, the girl has serious lungs. Abby continues to resist, tightly pressing her lips together. "She never wants to eat her breakfast." "What is it?" "Strained apricots" She answers. That's why. The mushy food, with small strands of apricot sprouting out of it, looks slimy on the spoon and the orange-ish color isn't too appealing either. Aunt Kerry sighs. "Ok Abby you don't have to eat this." She places the lid back on the jar. Abby stops whining and sits still. Instead, Aunt Kerry makes oatmeal. It looks considerably better than the apricots, not much. Abby seems to enjoy it. She swallows small spoonfuls-- thin streams of oatmeal sliding down her tiny round chin. "Would you like some Amelia?" She points to the pot. "Oh, no I'm fine." I sit down at the kitchen table. "How'd you sleep?" She looks at me while feeding Abby. "Um, I didn't have the best night." "I'm sure it will get better once you get used to the house." She softly wipes Abby's chin with her bib. Aunt Kerry offers me two other breakfast delights-- applesauce with figs or a carrot-nut-raisin muffin. I reject both offers. "You've got to eat something. What about toast and jam?" "Yeah that's fine." You can never go wrong with toast. Aunt Kerry has her back to me and Abby while she pulls two slices of bread from a bag. Abby's staring at me. Her large brown eyes are intense. I stare back. I can't believe I'm having a stare-off with an eleven month old. Mature, I know. My eyes begin to sting, that same familiar feeling at the diner. Abby's eyes enlarge and she parts her mouth to let out a cry. I press the side of my finger against my lips. "Shhh, don't cry."I whisper. The small oak-framed mirror hung on the wall show my eyes turn goldenly clear. Abby screams and Aunt Kerry jumps. "Abby what's wrong?" She turns to the highchair and begins to inspect her. I quickly go to the living room. Great I scared her. I'm scaring myself. Just, calm down. I close my eyes, breathing deeply. When I return, Abby is calmed down, her face tear stained. Aunt Kerry puts the toast in the oven. "There's some juice in the refrigerator." She gives me a glass. I pour a glass of apple juice and take a sip. It's unsweetened.

Gross. Later she places a plate on the table with my toast on it. Apparently, you can go wrong with toast. "Sorry about that Amelia, I should have put the timer on." She scrapes burnt flakes onto the plate. I drench the toast in strawberry jam and eat it. Tomorrow, I'm making my own toast. After breakfast I clean up in a different bathroom on the main floor. This one isn't so scarily white and a lot larger. The walls are painted a light-tawny color and its earth toned décor and wooden fixtures complement each other well. I like it. I grab a pale brown towel hanging on the rack when I step out the shower. I dry off quickly and limp back to my room. I sit down and rub my ankle-- it still hurts, badly. I'm not sure how I'm going to hide the pain or the hobbling. All I can do is hope Aunt Kerry doesn't notice. I comb through my hair after I finish pulling on jeans and tank-top. Downstairs, Abby is caught in a trance watching a brightly- colored cartoon. I slide onto the couch and watch it with her. Luckily she doesn't notice me or she might start crying again. The odd-shaped, multi colored character starts dancing and so does Abby. I'm twisting my cell phone around in my hand. Maybe I should text him. No, don't. He doesn't deserve a text from you. I battle with myself as I lie on the couch trying to make a decision to text or not to text. Aunt Kerry walks in, I didn't even notice her. "Amelia" she laughs "you don't have to watch this with Abby. There's cable in your room." "No, its fine, I don't mind." She laughs again. "Okay." I decide not to text. The day was lazy which is okay with me. I took a self-tour through the house, neatly braided my hair in two long French braids, and played some games on the computer. In the midday, Abby started to warm up to me. Actually she warmed up towards the chocolate chip cookie she noticed in my hand. Now it's 7:45 and dark outside. Abby's lying in her play pen, sleeping. My stomach grumbles. I'm hungry but I'm afraid of what's for dinner, remembering my tasty breakfast. The doorbell rings and Aunt Kerry answers it. "Have a good night." She says seconds later as she balances a large flat box on one hand and closes the door with the other. Pizza, thank God. "Amelia, dinner's here." I follow her into the kitchen. She passes me a plate and a napkin. I take two slices and sit down, she sits across from me. I can tell she wants to talk about something because she takes a bite of pizza, looks up at me, and then looks back at her pizza. "Amelia." I knew it. "Yes?" "How is it with just you and your mom?" I shrug. "I liked it better with my dad." Aunt Kerry nods. "Liam was very sweet. He treated your mom like a princess." She smiles. Yeah, that was the problem. I continue to eat. "Your mom told me you guys were going through a rough patch, with the loss of your dad, and still having to move to a new place, his old home, without him." "Well, he wanted to move there and my mom wanted to honor him, plus they already paid a down payment for it. So, might as well." I bitterly retort. Aunt Kerry clears her throat and smiles weakly. "I'm sure it will get better for you and your mom. It's just going to take time." I shrug and put the half-eaten slice back on the plate. Talk about killing an appetite "I think I'm going to go to bed." I push the chair back and start walking towards the staircase. "Are you sure? There's a lot of pizza here." She tries to get me to come back. "Yeah, I'm sure." I pull myself onto the bed. I think about my dad... and my mom. How it was better for both of us when he was here. Dad was like a balance. And now that he's gone, mom and I are...unleveled. Aunt Kerry said it will get better but I don't know if I can believe that.

Chapter 12

I hear that sound again. This time it sounds like it's in the room. I get up, painfully balancing on my tip toes, towards the closet. I reach for the handle and twist it. My phone buzzes off the table. I jump and take a deep slow breath. I pick up my phone--one missed call from Zev. "Why won't you stop calling me?" I whisper. "Because…" I spin around, ready to scream and he covers my mouth. "I miss you." He's pressing his other hand onto my back. I'm staring into his eyes, the same translucent color mine have been changing to. Zev moves his hand away from my mouth slowly. And for a brief moment I want to kiss his lips and press my body deeper into his embrace. But out of fear and surprise I start to punch him in his chest. "Hey!" he quietly exclaims "stop hitting me." "What are you doing here?!" "Listen, ok, I need to explain some things to you." I cross my arms over my chest. "How did you know where I am? Are you a stalker now?" He lifts his eyebrow and slightly scrunches his nose. He's so cute. Lia, get a hold of yourself. "I'm not even going to answer that." He thrusts his hands into his pockets. "So let me get this straight. You drove for hours to tell me "some things"." I make air quotes. "You know there's this thing called texting..." He interjects "I've been texting you. You never answered one of them." I put my phone back on the table. "I snuck in the attic last night and since then have been trying to decide if I should wait until you get back to the Falls or just tell you now." I look at him. "That was you?! You were making those sounds. And that *was* you I saw in the window!" I lean towards him. He leans back and smiles. "Please, don't hit me again." I roll my eyes. "I don't care what you have to tell me. You need to leave. Climb down the same way you climbed up…" I push him towards the window. "… and get in your car and drive back home." I open the window. He pushes his hands on the window frame to stop me from pushing anymore. "I didn't drive my car." Zev turns to face me. "Then how did you get here?" He grabs my arms, pulls me into a hug, and begins to scale down the wall. I close my eyes tight. Being upside down, rapidly scaling down a three-story house, head first, is not the best view. When Zev reaches the ground he begins to sprint on all fours. I'm clasping his neck with my arms, my legs wrapped around his waist, my face pressed against his chest. The ground scrapes my back. I can feel rips in my t-shirt and small cuts being made in my back. I want him to stop. This ride is painful and I want to get off. I try to scream his name but I can't even yell. He's running so fast the air doesn't allow me to catch my breath. He finally stops. My eyes are still closed tight and I'm not releasing my death grip. "Lia?" he tries to unwind my arms from around his neck. "We've stopped." I open my eyes and drop from him. I get up and brush some of the leaves and dirt off me. My heart is racing. I stare at him while I take slow steps backward. "What…are you?" I stare at him. His amber eyes glisten. "Lia, we need to talk." "No, we don't. I don't talk to weird guys that scale down houses and run on all fours." I keep backing up. "That's the only way you would come with me. If I tried to ask you, you'd have said no." `Zev steps closer. I step back. "We really need to talk Lia. I'm only trying to protect you." "Protect me, from what?" "People and..." I interject. "At the moment the only person I need protection from is you." I turn and dart into the wooded backdrop. I don't even know where I am. I keep running anyway, my ankle is in pain, I ignore it. I can hear leaves being rustled and sticks snapping. Zev is running a few trees away from me. My winded running compared to his pant-free jog. It's like he's not even out of breath. I know I can't outrun him but I'm going to try. I pick up my pace. He picks his up too. I look over again and Zev is clearing logs and trees-- moving and jumping over them effortlessly. Suddenly I fall on my stomach paired with a terrifying shriek. I look down and my foot is caught in a twisted tree root. I grab at my ankle-- the same ankle that has been hurting for the past day. It feels like it's going to snap. I start wiggling my foot and pull my body forward. I yank my foot free and start running again. Seconds later I fall and tumble down a slight hill, my ankle is too weak. Zev jumps on top of me. His teeth larger and way more pointed than I remember, his amber eyes burning into mine. "Are you ready to talk now?" Zev's usually silky tone is gruff and raspy. I slowly shake my head yes. I'm afraid to answer otherwise.

Chapter 13

Zev props me up against a tree and then rests my ankle on his thigh. I grimace. He rips the bottom of his t-shirt and firmly wraps my ankle. He starts to examine the sole of my foot and abruptly removes a piece of twig lodged into it. I scream. Zev stares at me. "You should have put on shoes." "You shouldn't have dragged me out of the house!" Zev backs up and smiles softly. "You are one." "I'm one what?!" "Your eyes are glowing." He keeps his stare constant at my eyes. I look away. "I don't know what you're talking about." Zev pulls my chin softly until I'm facing him again. "It's okay." I push his hand away. "I don't know what you're talking about, so leave me alone. I don't want to see you any more, Zev." I scratch the tree bark with my fingernails trying to pull myself up. I lean against it. I keep any weight off my ankle by keeping my leg bent and hop to the closest tree. Already, I'm out of breath. I've hopped three trees away and Zev is steadily behind me. "Leave me alone!" I stop and balance on my one leg. Instantly he's standing in front of me. He presses his hand against the tree, his arm blocking my path. "I know about your dad." "You don't know anything about him." I slap his arm down and continue to hobble. "I know that he was like me…a wolf."

That makes me stop and grab a tree for support. "What?" I stare at his face in the darkness. He steps closer. "You expect me to believe that?" Even though for a second I did. Come on Lia, that's ridiculous. I roll my eyes and turn away. Zev grabs my elbow. "Had he ever explained his childhood to you? Where he grew up, how he grew up?" "No. It's not like it mattered. He always told me his childhood was in the past and that's where it going to stay. And I never minded that answer." I snatch my elbow away. "Don't you ever feel weird?" "Don't you ever leave a person alone?" I shamble to the next tree. At this rate I should be out of these woods in six months. "You never feel a burning sensation throughout your body." I swallow hard. I feel him rush behind me and squeeze my waist. He whispers. "You have, haven't you?" I'm getting scared now, like completely freaking out. "I can smell your fear." His minty warm breath exhales onto my ear. "I'm not scared." I whisper, closing my eyes. Zev's rhythmic breathing moves down to my neck. I can feel his chest expanding and contracting against my back. I keep my eyes closed not wanting to lose this feeling. "You should be." He rips away from me snapping me from my trance. I whip around to only see darkness. No Zev in sight. "I'm a bad guy Lia." My eyes dart to the trees. I scarcely make him out perched upon a thick branch. "There are things I've done or tried to do." "What things? What are you talking about?" My voice echoes amongst the trees. In the next instant he's standing in front of me, I didn't even see him move from the tree. I gasp and trip backwards. He catches me before I reach the ground. "I thought you said you weren't scared." I don't answer. I only try to calm my quickening heart.

☽

The silver crescent moon is draped in a soft glow. He's staring at it-- his amber eyes are smoldering. Narrow streams of steam escape his pupils. We're sitting against a large tree with even larger roots. My heart is pumping so fast it has to be dangerous. Relax Lia. Take a breath. "Calm down." He slightly turns to me. If he only knew that I'm trying to. He softly places his hand over my heart. "It's okay. Don't be scared." "I'm not." I lie while gently pulling his hand from my over my heart. "Why did you say you were a "bad guy"?" "Because…" He looks down "…what I tried to do…to you." Confusion blankets my face. "Are you talking about that night at the cabin?" "Yes." "I tried to forget what you did to me Zev and you're making it difficult." "Do you even remember what happened?" Zev faces me completely. "It's pretty obvious what happened. Taking me to that abandoned cabin, drugging me with cider, and then I wake up the next morning feeling the worst I ever have." "Lia what you're thinking is not what happened!" He snaps. "I would never do that to any girl!" Zev stands over me. I widely open my eyes, looking up to him. He quickly calms his anger and bends down until we're eye level. "Lia I…I…" Zev stands up and turns away. I pull myself up and grab his shoulder. "What? Tell me what happened that night. I've been confused since then. I've been thinking one horrible thing and you're telling me something else. Just tell me." "I tried to kill you that night." My hand drops from his shoulder. I stumble backwards. Images foggily race through my mind-- the cabin, the fire, the cider, Zev watching while I'm being dragged by my legs, fighting wolves. I feel my body slam back against the tree. I vaguely see Zev approach me. My eyes begin to close and I feel him jerk on my shoulders. "Lia?" The last thing I hear before darkness.

CHAPTER 14

An intense white light is shining in my face. I turn away from it and the light finds my face again. "It looks like she's waking up. Amelia, can you hear me?" A deep voice loudly questions. I weakly whine while I cover my eyes with my forearm. The light goes off and I drop my forearm slowly opening my eyes. "Amelia? Honey, are you okay?" Aunt Kerry rests her hand on my forehead. "She should be getting better." A tall lean man with short red hair and a matching cropped goatee writes on a chart. "You were asleep for quite a while." "The bright light always seems to make the patient "come to the light"." He jokes. My aunt smiles and keeps her attention on me. "I'll make sure she gets plenty of fluids and antibiotics. The fever should break in no time." "Thank you, Doctor." He smiles at my aunt as he exits the room. "Where am I?" I lift my head from the pillow and look around. "You're at Blessed Hearts Hospital." "Why am I here, what happened?" "I went to wake you up and you were sweating, hot, and your ankle was very swollen." I look down at my thickly bandaged ankle. It feels better, finally. "Luckily, your ankle was only fractured and not broken." Yes, that's some luck. "I called your mom. She was here all day yesterday, she refused to leave." Aunt

Kerry caresses my hair. "She's going to be so happy to see that you woke up. She's down at the cafeteria." "Yesterday…how long have I been here?" "Two days." Surprised, I sink my head back into the pillow and stare at the tiled ceiling. "Amelia?" My mom rushes to my bedside and kisses my forehead. "I'm so glad you're awake, I was so worried." My mom places the sandwiches and juices on a chair. My eyebrows are lifted in shock as she cups my face with her hands and kisses my cheek. I've never seen my mom act like this before, not behind me anyways. "How do you feel?" "I feel okay." She rubs my hand, the IV is gently pulled. I wince and my hand retracts. "I'm sorry sweetie." She softly pats the IV and moves her hand. Aunt Kerry grabs a sandwich and starts to unwrap the plastic covering. She hands one to my mom who does the same. "I bought an extra one, its ham. Are you hungry?" Of course she would forget I hate ham. "No." I answer pulling the blanket up. Mom takes a couple small bites of the compact ham sandwich before wrapping it back up. Aunt Kerry is facing the TV watching a celebrity news show. I scan the room. It's more sterile than Aunt Kerry's bathroom. I didn't even think that was possible. The constant beeping monitor next to my bed is getting on my nerves and that ill, pine-sol-ish smell is making me queasy. Somebody needs to either give me something to knock me out or release me. I can only tolerate a hospital room for so long. "When can I get out of here?" "The doctor said as soon as your fever breaks." Aunt Kerry places her hand back on my forehead. "The last temperature reading was 102 degrees. Three degrees lower than yesterday. It's a miracle that you're even awake." Mom adds while she sits in the chair next to the bed and pulls out a bulky book from her bag. "You should get some rest, okay." She kindly suggests as she opens her book and turns to where the bookmark is wedged. I don't want to rest I want to get out of here. The heat permeates through my skin. I look at my bandaged ankle and the IV taped to my hand. I guess there's no use in putting up a fight. I watch the news show with Aunt Kerry until I fall asleep.

☽

"96.9. Perfect." I feel a slender stick being pulled from my mouth. "It seems that someone is well enough to go home." The same red-haired doctor smiles and pulls my eyelids open as he quickly flashes light onto them. I blink a couple times to make the colored spots disappear. I pull my head up from the pillow. The TV's off and Aunt Kerry's gone. My mom is standing on the other side of the bed, in a different outfit. The doctor sits down on the edge of the bed and adjusts his small-frame glasses. "We were getting worried there Amelia. You fell into a coma with your fever. But three days later you're awake with no fever in sight. That's phenomenal." He chuckles and writes on his chart. "You're definitely healthy enough to go home. Just take it easy on your ankle. For assistance we have some crutches available for you." He pulls them from the corner and does a demonstration. His imbalance on the crutches causes him to lurch forward. "Well hopefully you will have a better command of them than I do." I laugh softly. "I think I will." "Thanks, Doctor Redding." Mom smiles and pats my hand. "It's no problem." He returns the smile and props the crutches back against the wall. The door softly clicks as he closes it. "He's such a nice doctor." She sits on the bed. "Well it looks like we can go home." Mom pushes her book back in her bag. "We? What happened to staying with Aunt Kerry?" "Oh, I told her I'd think it'd be best if I took you home and cared for you." She grabs a huge fuzzy white bear with a large purple heart stitched onto its chest. "Aunt Kerry got this for you from the gift shop. Isn't it cute?" Mom turns and places it back on the table. "Yeah, it's cute." I sit up and a smaller brown bear rolls forward. I laugh. "How many bears did Aunt Kerry buy me?" My mom turns to face me. "That's not from your aunt. I went to the bathroom a few minutes ago and when I came back it was next to you." I stare at it and place it on the table next to the other bear. "Ok honey, let's get you up." I wrap my arm around my mom's neck as she firmly holds my waist pushing me up. "Good thing you only weigh like a hundred pounds or this might be really difficult. "I do not." I respond defensively. She laughs as she continues to help me up. "It's only a joke Amelia." Once I'm up I balance by holding on to the bed bars. "I didn't think you were going to heal so fast…" She shuffles through a small plastic bag. "Sorry about that." I lean against the bed. Mom lifts her eyebrow. "I see sickness doesn't take away sarcasm." She hands me the pajamas I was wearing that night…with Zev. "What am I supposed to do with those?" "Put them on. I never left the hospital room and I didn't get a chance to get any other clothes." Mom tosses them onto the bed. "What about my suitcase?" "Have you seen how large that parking lot is? I am not walking all the way to the car to get a change of clothes when there's a perfectly good change right here." "Then I'd rather wear this hospital gown." "You can if you want if you don't mind everyone seeing your pretty flowery panties." I reach back and snatch the gown closed. My mom grabs my waist and the pajamas and helps me to the bathroom. I lean onto the countertop peering into the mirror, I look horrible. My eyes are puffy and red, my skin looks shallow, and my hair is a mess. Sigh. I don't even care. I just want to get out of here. Mom knocks on the door just as I'm pulling on my pajama shirt. I open the door and she helps me to the bed. "Here are your crutches." I pull one under each arm and stand up slowly. "Okay, let's go." She opens the door for me and walks behind me. "Amelia, I think I need to buy you new pajamas." I can feel her fingers run down the rips in the back of my t-shirt. "It looks like you've been dragged or something." "Yeah, I um…" I can't even think of an excuse for my shirt. Fortunately I don't have to because my mom's interest quickly goes to discussing a small clothing boutique in Wolf Falls that sells cotton pajamas. "There is a pink short set with tiny sheep all over them. Those were so cute." "Sheep?" My mom presses the down button and instantly the elevator doors ding open. We're in the elevator alone. My mom tries to balance her over-stuffed bag and my two big bears. She pulls her purse strap over her body, tucks the white bear under her arm, and holds the brown bear in her hands. She turns it around and plucks at the nose. "What a cute bear." She rubs her fingertips against the marble eyes. "Your father's eyes would change to that color sometimes." I stare at the bear's bright amber eyes. "When he would get upset or happy, I guess it was like an emotional-hormonal thing, I don't know." Her eyes tear up and she turns the bear down. I look away and balance on my crutches. It's not the most comfortable thing to see my mom upset. I watch the numbered buttons illuminate quickly as we go from the fourth floor down to the first floor. When the doors open my mom motions for me to step out of the elevator first because she's fumbling through her bag searching for the car key; which means I don't have the extra help to balance. I try to walk forward and I can't seem to gain coordination. I'm sure at this point I don't look any better than the doctor's demonstration.

Chapter 15

I've been home for almost two weeks and I've been in bed for a good portion of it. I only get up to shower and then it's back to sleeping. Zev hasn't texted me since I've been in the hospital. And I guess that's a good thing. I guess. I'll eat lunch with my mom today. It's better than eating in my room, alone. I pull the crutches under my arms and slowly make it down the steps. Metrically, my body slightly swings as I step with the crutches. "Finally got the hang of it Amelia?" Mom smiles as she slides an enchilada onto a plate. "I was just coming up there with your lunch." "I wanted to eat down here for a change." I pull the chair out and slide onto it. "How's the ankle?" "It's good." I wiggle my toes. She places the plate in front of me and sits across from me with her helping. "So summer's officially here as of..." Mom pauses to peer at the calendar tacked to the wall. "...four days ago." I swirl the prongs of my fork in the sauce. "What are you going to do?" "Well with an injured ankle probably not much." I lick sauce off the prongs. Mom sighs and begins to cut through her enchilada. "What about Zev?" I pause, fork in mid-air. "What about him?" "I haven't seen him anymore and you haven't been talking about him lately." I put my fork down and shrug. "We're just friends."

"You two should hang out this summer. Go do something fun." That sounds like a great idea, go and hang out with a guy who has tried to kill me. "It was just a thought." She notes my obvious tension I built from her suggestion. After I finish my serving I'm ready to go back to bed. "You don't want anymore?" Mom points to the short enchilada-filled pan. "No, I just want to take a shower, put on clean pajamas and go to bed." "That reminds me!" She jumps up, rushes to the living room, and returns seconds later holding a large white box with a bow wrapped around it. "I picked them up for you yesterday from the boutique." Please don't let them be those sheep covered pajamas. Please. I untie the ribbon and pull the lid off. "I told you they were cute." She smiles and points to the tiny sheep. "Thanks mom." At least I only have to sleep in them.

☽

I pull myself onto the bed, carefully propping my ankle onto a pillow. The brown bear from the hospital is leaning on my side table. I pick it up and pull it against my stomach. "Where'd you come from?" I turn the bear to face me as if it's going to answer. I squeeze its plush stomach and my thumb slides into a slit. A folded sheet of paper is stuffed inside. I pull it out, put the bear aside, and unfold it.

Dear Lia,

I'm sorry for everything I caused and everything I tried to do. It's before I got to know you. This may sound crazy but you changed my way of thinking. I'm trying to learn how to let things go. Like your dad told you, the past should stay in the past. He was right. I think it's best if we stay apart, I don't want to this situation to become any more complicated. I'm sorry.

-Zev

I ball the letter up and toss it across the room. I don't even know why I'm so upset. I mean why do I care? He admitted to trying to hurt me and I should be glad that he doesn't want to hang out or talk anymore. But, I'm not. Despite that admission, there's still something about him that pulls me in. That something that makes my heart beat uncontrollably when I see him or hear his name. I bite my lower lip to stop it from quivering and suppress oncoming tears. I'm so confused. I feel like he's not telling me everything just bits and pieces and that's what bothers me most. I hate this feeling. I lie completely on my back and can feel a headache forming from the tear restraining. I hug the bear firmly against my chest as I turn on my side. A few tears escape and I wipe them away quickly. No use in crying, Lia. It just wasn't meant to be.

Chapter 16

"Amelia!" Mom calls from downstairs. "Get up! Don't waste your summer away in that room." Ugh, it's *my* summer I can do with it what I want. I pull the pillow over my head. Another two weeks has passed and my ankle is almost healed. I could get up and go do things, without my crutches, the only problem is I don't want to. "Amelia!" I pull the pillow from my head and sit up. I rub the purple-ish spot on my ankle where it's still bruised. "I'm up!" Zombie-like, I yank the covers back and walk downstairs. "She has awakened from the dead." My mom puts her arms up and slowly does the thriller dance. "Funny." I lean on the counter rubbing my face. Once my eyes adjust I notice she is wearing overalls, a brightly colored bandana, and tennis shoes. Her hip is pressed against a short narrow cart packed with an assortment of sponges, sprays, and towels. "Uh, why are you dressed like that?" Mom adjusts fastens a button at her waist. "I have a job." "A job, where?" "I'll be cleaning for Mrs. Howlman. You know, *Zev's* grandmother." She emphasizes his name. There goes my heart beating. "I know who Mrs. Howlman is." I scratch my neck nervously. "Why are you cleaning for her?" "Because she's a sweet old lady who can't do it herself anymore not to mention the hours are short and the pay is decent." She pulls her mug from the counter and begins to sip. "You can come and help me clean if you want." "No thanks." I quickly reply. She snorts while she continues to sip coffee. I start walking back to the staircase. "Headed back to bed, Amelia?" "Yes." "Okay well I'll be gone for awhile. I'll be walking there so I'm leaving my car key on the hook." "You're walking *that* far?" I ask in disbelief. "It's not *that* far plus the exercise is good." I lean against the wall as she places her mug in the sink and grabs the handle to her cleaning cart. She gives me a quick hug and waves goodbye as she walks down the graveled pathway. I lock the door and sluggishly step upstairs. I sit on the edge of my bed. Usually when I was bored I'd play with Jojo or take her for a walk. That's not possible. What to do? What to do? I take a shower, get dressed, and pull the car key from the hook. I'm sitting in the driveway with both my hands on the steering wheel, the car quietly humming. Okay so now what? Where do I go from here? I don't even know of any hangouts in this town. I barely know any of the people in this town. After minutes of arguing with myself, which to an outsider I probably looked slightly crazy, I decide to go to the pizzeria. The only place I know of.

☽

The small restaurant is crowded. I push my way through a huddle of guys to get to the counter. I order a large orange soda and push back through the cluster in search for a place to sit. I spot a small table in the corner. Perfect. I push my back up against the wall and twist the tip of the straw with my fingers. Apparently my mom's method of going out isn't working because I'm still bored just in a different setting. I finish the last sip of soda. Great, the only thing that kept my interest is all gone. I could get a refill but I really can't afford to pay for one. Sigh. Fifteen minutes past and subconsciously I begin to people watch, a favorite pastime of mine. A tall guy with a faux-hawk wearing extremely old converse is trying to talk to a short girl with long, wavy, red hair. She keeps denying him turning back around to her two friends that are laughing at the poor guy's situation. I think it might have something to do with his shoes. There's a big difference between vintage and decrepit. He shifts his weight, placing his left foot forward. Did I just see his big toe poke through? It's definitely the shoes. Against the opposite wall, at the pinball machine, an overly muscled guy wearing a skin-tight blue t-shirt jolts the entire component. He bangs his hip against the table trying to force the ball to stay away from any holes. Seconds later he screams at it and kicks the sides when his score blinks a zero. He plays another dollar's worth and scores another zero. He's so upset this time, I'm afraid he'll break it. Veins bulging out the sides of his neck, his face red with anger, he begins lifting the machine inches from the ground. "Daniel put it down and try again later!"The owner yells to him. Uh, try again? I don't think that's such a good idea. He growls, puts it down, and takes a cigarette out from his pants pocket. As he's walking out the door he passes a girl with long black hair and unmistakable green eyes; Aja. I sink down into my seat pulling my hood on. I watch her slide into an empty booth. She extends her arms across the table and spins her cell on the laminate. She's waiting for someone. I wonder who? Casually she looks out the window, down at her cell, then back out the window. After a couple repeats of this routine she begins to finger through her hair and hastily apply more lip-gloss. He coolly walks in dressed in white thermal and dark blue jeans. He runs his hand over his hair to smooth his waves. A few guys greet him as he pasts them. After stopping to exchange words he shoves his hands in his pockets and arrives to awaiting Aja. "Hey, Zev." She stands wrapping her arms around his neck. He pats her sides and breaks the hug. My widened eyes watch her softly peck his lips. He pulls back and slides into the booth. I can't believe this, he's dating her. She grabs his hands from across the table. I got to get out of here. I don't want to see anymore. I pull up from the chair and try to see if there's a clear path from here to the door without Zev or his new girl seeing me. "Pepperoni please" Aja happily answers as Zev slides out of the booth. Crap she just couldn't wait to order. How am I supposed to get out of here now? I can't past the counter without him seeing me. He leans up against the counter resting on his elbows. Just when I was thinking there was no escape, crazy pinball guy returns. "I'm ready to take you on." He flexes his muscles and points to the machine. He's just big enough for me to hide behind as I sneak out the door. I stay crouched until I get in the car. I can't believe it. They're going out. I should have known. Maybe I'm too mixed up for him. I guess he just likes a girl all of one race, not an Oreo or Zebra or whatever else I used to get called. Or maybe I have too many issues and he can read them all over my face. But he does too. He told me he's a wolf, just like my dad was. So if anyone has problems, it's definitely him. I tap the steering wheel with tips of my fingers while chewing on my bottom lip. I should go back in there and tell him off. And then I could get crazy pinball guy to beat him up for me. I sink back into the chair and think of different scenarios that all end with Zev in some kind of pain. I guess that's sort of psycho to even imagine. But he deserves it. Zev's mustang is parked right in the front of the restaurant. I'll just wait for the date to end and sneak over to his car. Hopefully I won't be seen. I want him to be totally surprised when he gets in to drive home and discovers me waiting to completely berate him. Forty-five minutes past. The sky is darkening the longer I sit here, I should leave. I start the car and turn it back off. No, I'll stay and tell Zev what I think about him and his new girl. No matter how long they take. The bells clank violently against the glass door. I jump up hitting my forehead against the visor. Crap. Zev's car is gone. There are only two cars, other than me, that remain in the parking lot-- a white VW that Aja drove and a gray truck. The owner checks the lock and pulls on the door handle before walking across the street to his car. I sit up and adjust my eyes to the darkness. I lean forward covering my mouth. I pull myself lower into my seat without breaking my stare. Aja's pressed against her car using pinball guy's body as the press. He's kissing her neck and she's rubbing his back. My eyes expand and my mouth parts in disbelief. Her eyes morph into that familiar amber color. Her nails grow long, jagged, and sharp. She scratches his back ripping through his t-shirt leaving open cuts. He leans back and lets out a deafening howl. I cover my ears quickly-- blood drips through my fingers. She laughs and pushes him away and begins to walk backwards into the street, teasingly leading him towards the woods with her index finger. "Come on." She instructs before turning around and disappearing into the thick trees. And of course, he follows. My first instinct is to call Zev. My second instinct is to bask in the glory of all that is payback. That's what he gets. But then I return to my first instinct. What would I tell him? How would I tell him? Would he think I'm a jealous girl who's making things up? I twist my phone around in my hand. The screen displays a bright 11:42 p.m. It's getting late. Whichever instinct I decide to carry out I better do it at home.

Chapter 17

The drive home is extremely dark except for the car's headlights. No streetlights, no porch lights, just darkness. This town is really starting to get under my skin. It's just weird. It's not even on a map. Mom and I found it based on some crazy directions my dad wrote. There's barely ever any sun, only constant rolling clouds. It's summer time and I have yet to see anything summer-y. No kids playing outside, no running through sprinklers, no obnoxious ice cream trucks. Everything just seems so bleak. I pull into the driveway and park. I have no idea why my dad raved over this place and why he *had* to move back. It's nowhere I'd want to be. Even though, unfortunately, I am. I fall on my bed face first. I don't even take anything off but my shoes. I let my face immerse deep into the softness of the pillow. My pillow is laced with my shampoo's strawberry-melon scent. It smells good. My face is so deep into the pillow I can't breathe. I close my eyes and let the fruity fumes go to my head. Maybe I'll pass out and wake up out of this town, perhaps back at Blessed Hearts. Which even if I'm feeling better I'll fake that I'm not so I'll have to stay. And I can be out of this town, at least for awhile. That idea seems perfect until I start to choke. I turn on my back and unzip my hoodie.

I stare up at the ceiling until I can't anymore. I lie on my side and try to sleep. But all I can do is think about Zev, Aja, and what I saw. I turn the other way and pull my knees up to my chest, then I turn on my back with my legs straight out, next I turn on my stomach with my arms and legs wildly stretched. I just can't get into a comfortable position. I take a couple deep breaths and slowly sing the alphabet. When I couldn't sleep my dad used to sing it to me. It would always lull me to sleep by the time he got to N. I was like five then but it's worth a try. When I reach P I can feel my body relaxing and my eyes becoming heavy. It still works.

☽

"Of course I will. Have a good day. Bye" My mom places the phone back in its charger. "Who was that?" I yawn. "Amelia." She jumps and fingers through her blonde hair. "You're up early. It's not even six am yet." "I couldn't really sleep." I sit down on the sofa next to my mom. "That was Daniel Smith's mother. He never came home last night and she wanted the community to keep an eye out for him." "Daniel?" "Yes." Crazy pinball guy. "His mother is worried, as I would be. I heard two teenagers have already gone missing in the past month or so. I think their names were Samuel and Dan-" "Dante?" I finish her sentence. She softly grabs her neck. "Yes. It's so scary. You would think in a small town like this things like that wouldn't happen." Mom pats my thigh. "When you go out, please be careful and aware." "I will." I answer while thinking about Daniel. She kisses my forehead and gets up. "I'm going to go back to bed." I'm trying not to think the worst but how could I not. In a small town like this, who just disappears? It has to have something to do with Aja. That's the last person I saw Daniel with. I begin to chew on my bottom lip-- my thinking habit. Does she have something to do with those other disappearances? What if Zev disappears next? I have to tell him my synopsis on his girlfriend. He has to know what I saw. But how do I tell him without seeming… crazy? I need to tell him in person, so the cell phone option is out. I'll walk over to his house, knock on the door, and tell him we need to talk. No, that's so random. I need a reason to be there other than to tell him about Aja the destroyer. "I need a way to tell him." I say aloud. As if to answer my frustration a sponge falls off from mom's cleaning cart, plopping against the floor. I hate cleaning. But if that's the only way to warn him then that's what I'll do.

Chapter 18

I didn't even go back to sleep. I went upstairs, took a shower, dressed in sweats, and now I'm sitting on the counter anxiously waiting for my mom. I hear a door open and the steps begin to creak. She clicks the light on and puts her hand over heart. "Amelia, I swear you're going to give me a heart attack. Why are you sitting in the kitchen in the dark?" Mom turns on the coffee maker. "I was waiting to tell you that I want to go with you today…to uh help you clean." I run my fingernail in between the white tiles. "What a surprise." She smiles. "I could use the extra help." I quickly return the smile and look away. I hope she can't see through that lie to my real intentions. "Would this sudden urge to help have anything to do with seeing Zev?" Her smile turns sly with a slight eyebrow lift. Does she have X-ray vision? "No, of course not, I just wanted to help. There's nothing else to do in this town." I twist the tip of my ponytail around my finger. Mom nods and pulls down a mug for coffee. An hour later we're driving to Mrs. Howlman's house. My mom is talking to me about cleaning the back porch or something, I don't really hear her. My mind is solely focused on Zev. I mean it's solely focused on exactly how and what I'll tell him about Aja. I'm not just thinking only about him. Never mind. I softly rub my forehead and turn the heat releasing vent towards me. "It's cooler than usual today?" She softly turns a corner and continues straight. "Yeah it is." I zip my hoodie up to my neck and slide my hands into the pockets. "There's a lot of house to clean but we'll just tackle it room by room." Mom drives onto the pathway and parks. I exit the car quickly, walking up the steps to the front door. I knock and wait for an answer. I can hear gentle scuffles approaching the front door. "Good morning Mrs. Howlman." "Amelia, how nice?" she smiles and adjusts her glasses. "You're helping your mother clean today?" "Yes." "That's sweet of you. Come in, I was just cooking breakfast." I step inside and mom trails behind me with her cart. I unzip my hoodie and take a breath. It's so overly warm. Mrs. Howlman comes from the kitchen carrying a small bowl of bubbling, lumpy, gray-ish liquid. I think its oatmeal, although I'm not too sure. "You two should come eat before you start to clean." She sits the bowl on the table next to a place setting. Mom and I exchange the same disgusting look and we both, politely, deny her offer. Mom started to clean the living room and sent me to the back porch. I really don't want to clean but I have to keep my cover until I can talk to Zev. I open the French doors slowly and a cloud of dust is released. I cover my mouth while fanning the grimy air. It looks like this porch hasn't been used in some years. Thick cobwebs drape from the awning, the rusting patio furniture are amiss amongst the random junk and boxes piled high. Where do I even begin? I take my bandana off and tie it over my nose and mouth. Now that I can breathe I can concentrate on how to clean up this mess. I begin to stack the boxes on top of each other. Once some boxes are out of the way I reach for a busted antique table lamp. I try to pick it up and it's heavier than I thought. I try again and attempt number two isn't any better-- I still can't pick it up. I grab its neck and lean my body back. I can't believe I'm in a tug-of-war with a lamp. I grab its chord and begin to pull and instantly I can feel less resistance. As soon as I yank its chord free, the stack of boxes completely tumbles. I pick up the portion of the chord that was stuck underneath the stack; no wonder I couldn't lift the lamp. I look at the overturned boxes. All contents that were inside are now scattered across the porch floor. Great, more work for me. I kneel down and pick up the pictures putting them back in a box. The last picture falls on top of the pile. I pause and lift it slowly. There are three people-- they look like they're my age, all squeezed on the couch in Mrs. Howlman's living room, I can tell because nothing's changed. The girl is holding a baby leaning into a guy that's identical to Zev and next to him is…my dad. "I look like him, huh?" I twist around. "Zev!" He stands over me. I stand up with the picture still in hand. Zev pulls my hand up and looks at the picture. "You look like your dad too." Zev's eyes move from the picture to my face. "I didn't know that my dad knew your parents." "Why would you? He didn't want to talk about the past, right? Isn't that what you said?" "Yes but-" He interrupts. "Well then you wouldn't know anything he did…all the bad things." My face twists into confusion. "Bad things, what are you talking about?" He scoffs and moves some boxes out of his path. "I was hoping we would barely see each other. But for some reason you keep showing up everywhere I am. Like yesterday, at the pizzeria." He folds his arms over his chest staring intently. "I can go where I want Zev, how I was supposed to know that you and your new girlfriend from hell were going to be there." Momentarily, he looks away, like mentioning her makes his skin crawl. "She's real cool. I've decided that we should give each other a chance." Now that makes my skin crawl. "Cool? You think so? I've seen some things that she's done that aren't so cool." Disbelief blankets his face. "Like what?" "Well Daniel disappeared…" "Yeah, so, everyone knows he gets too drunk to make it home some nights he's probably passed out somewhere. What's your point?" "Well I saw him…with Aja the night before at the pizzeria." He shoves his hands into his pockets and leans against the paneled wall. "I never took you for a liar." "I'm not lying. I saw them together that night." "*That night*, Lia, after we ate Aja had to go home to care for her dad." "How do you know she wasn't lying? Have you met her dad?" "You're ridiculous." Zev walks through the double doors into the living room. I follow him. "Zev wait-" "Lia!" Angrily, he turns around. "Stop trying to talk to me, leave me alone. Just be a coward and give up, like your dad." I redden his cheek with a hard slap and push past him. I'm not even sure why he said that about my dad but still it's hurtful. I rush outside crashing into Mrs. Howlman. She drops her watering can and grabs hold of the post and I grab her other arm. "I'm so sorry." I breathily say, trying to stop any tears from coming. "It's alright dear." She lifts my chin slowly. "What's wrong?" "Nothing." "It looks like something to me." Mrs. Howlman slowly lowers herself onto the swing and pats the empty spot next to her. "If it's about Zev, don't be upset, ever since his friends went missing he hasn't been the same ever since." Being reminded about the disappearances dampers my already saddened attitude. I take a deep breath and sit down, teary-eyed, still holding the picture. She softly pulls it from my hand and smiles. "I remember that day." She cleans her glasses lens with the hem of her dress and slides them back on. "Paul, Vanessa and your dad went out to spend the day together." As Mrs. Howlman tells me the story behind the picture, mental images begin to flash. "See, Paul and Vanessa had Zev when they were seventeen. And of course a baby changes a lot of things. They couldn't go out like they used to. So I told them I'd watch Zev and they can go out and have a good time." The more she tells me the weirder I feel. I close my eyes and feel a violent rush flow through my body. I quickly open my eyes and I'm still at Mrs. Howlman's house, but something's different. I jump off the swing and glance around quickly. My mom's car that was parked in front of the porch is gone and so is Zev's classic mustang. I call for my mom but no sound leaves my mouth. I grab my throat and try again. No success. The door opens and Vanessa, Paul and my dad are walking down the front porch, waving goodbye to Mrs. Howlman and a newly born Zev. I follow behind them, picking up my pace. "It's going to be so fun." Paul playfully pulls Vanessa by the waist. She giggles and accepts his embrace. "Liam, when are you going to get a girlfriend and stop being the third wheel?" Paul reaches over and slaps my dad's shoulder. "Please, I'm too young to be tied down to somebody." "Yeah, okay. You'll be the next one with a baby, probably next year." Paul jokes, kissing Vanessa's cheek. "Having a baby at eighteen? I don't think so." Well you were wrong about that one dad. I keep my pace close trying to hear every word. "So what are we going to do?" Vanessa buttons her denim jacket. "I say we go get something to eat and play some arcade games." Dad zips his jacket and puts his hands in the pockets. Paul and Vanessa agree. Zev looks so much like his dad, it's uncanny. I noticed the resemblance in the picture but it doesn't do justice compared to seeing him in the flesh. I quickly go to the opposite side of the trio and walk next to my dad. His looks never changed and neither did his likeable personality. Seeing him makes me miss him even more. They stop at a crosswalk waiting for the line of cars to pass. Given the opportunity, I step closer to my dad with my arms out, in an attempt to hug him and they ghost through him. I keep trying and my arms continue to swat the air. They begin to cross the street and I follow. I wish I could have gotten one last hug. The fifteen minute walk ends at the pizzeria. Vanessa and Paul pick a booth while dad goes to order. They joke, laugh, eat, and play games for hours. After the third pizza, Vanessa's leans her head on her hand and looks at her watch on the opposite wrist. "We should get going. It's getting late." Paul and my dad exchange looks. "No, please mommy, don't make us go home yet." They simultaneously beg, clasping their hands together. She laughs. "Okay, one more hour, and then we should go home. I miss Zev." They each take their soda and leave the restaurant. "What now?" Vanessa walks along a concrete beam. Paul slurps his drink. "I don't know." "Let's go to the Ravine." Dad suggests, his eyes widening. "I don't know, man. We shouldn't really be going over there." "Come on. We could go for a night swim and then home." "That sounds fun." Vanessa lightly tugs Paul's jacket. "Come on, let's do it." He smiles at her, "alright." They turn around and begin to walk into the same wooded area across from the pizzeria that I saw Aja lead Daniel into. Their walk turns into a fast-paced race going deeper and deeper into the woods. A large cliff stops their dash. They exchange looks, their amber eyes glowing in the darkness and suddenly they jump. I rush to the edge, horrified. And that's when I see it, mid-air. My dad and his friends' bodies contort and twist, changing into wolves. Howls cut through the quiet night air. My dad lands on his back and whimpers like a dog. As quickly as they morphed into a wolf they turn back to their original form. I'm mortified, I don't even know what to think or do. I lean over the edge, watching intently. My dad balances on his knees slowly rubbing his lower back. Paul pushes him back down as he rushes past him heading for the stream. Vanessa follows, jumping on Paul's back which results in both of them crashing into the water. "Come on Liam." Vanessa wades in the water, motioning for my dad to join in their swim. "Okay, okay, I'm coming." He runs to the shoreline and a gunshot is fired. Paul pulls Vanessa out of the water as they all quickly scramble back to the cliff. They begin to climb. A closer gunshot is fired and it chips the rock my dad was using as support. I'm so engrossed I don't realize I'm getting ready to topple over edge, until I do. I get up and a heavy-set man runs closer, gun in hand, he stops, aims, and shoots. Luckily, it's another miss. His appearance becomes clearer the closer he gets-- short black hair, goatee, and green eyes. He's wearing a familiar leather jacket-- The Seekers stitched on the back. Once he finds his footing my dad begins to effortlessly scale the wall, pulling himself atop the cliff. "Hurry up." He gives his hands as support for Vanessa to use. Her fingers are inches away from my dad's palms. As hard as she tries a connection can't be made. "Reach a little more Vanessa." Over half of my dad's body has no support and if he leans over anymore he'll go over the edge. "I'm trying but I can't move. My foot is caught." Paul tries to untangle her foot from the twisted twine. After detangling and a push from Paul, Vanessa is finally able to grab my dad's hand. A third gunshot is fired and this time it doesn't miss. A large hole is made in her chest. Her eyes blink slowly, her mouth parts open, and her slender hand slips from my dad's grip. She falls from the cliff and lands on her back, a pool of blood forming around her. My eyes are as wide as my dad's. "Vanessa!" Paul screams. "Paul! Paul! We have to go." My dad's knees can't even hold him steady he's shaking so much. Tears quickly wet his cheeks. "Paul, man, I don't want to lose you too." My dad reaches for his hand. The hunter fires another gunshot that rips through Paul's forearm. He releases a deafening howl and drops back down to the muddy ground. His riotous demeanor paired with his wolf form only makes the hunter excited. "Its wolf hunting season, did you know that?" He cocks his large shotgun, spits on the ground, and keeps his gun aimed. "I like it when I get a challenge." His smile grows wide showing all of his teeth. I'm standing right in the middle of a war. The gun looks like it's aimed right between my eyes. Paul's breathing heavy and he's wounded. His tired and sad gaze keeps going to Vanessa. "I only got one silver bullet left." He gives a sideways smile. "It's just hard to figure out whether to put it in your chest or right through that dog brain of yours." Paul just stares, his fist balled tight, and jaw clenched. I wish I could do something. I wish I could help. Separate footsteps are made behind the hunter. A girl, maybe five, grab holds of his knee and smiles big. Aja?! Her black hair and vibrant green eyes are unmistakable, even as a child. "You want to take a shot?" He asks. She looks up and shakes her head yes. "Here, let daddy help you." He kneels down behind her, placing her finger over his on the trigger. Her eyes glow amber as they apply pressure to the trigger. As soon as the gun is fired my dad leaps down from the cliff landing on top of the hunter. Aja screams, falls back, and slices her elbow on a jagged rock. My dad turns the hunter on his back and gruesomely rips his chest open--snatching his heart out. Aja's intensely staring at the bloody pumping heart thrown inches away from her. "Daddy?" She whispers while crawling over to the heartless hunter. My dad throws the gun in the water and rushes over to Paul. His heroic effort was too late. The right side off Paul's face is completely... gone. Bloody, shaking, and scared my dad climbs back up the cliff and begins speedily running on all fours. I try to keep up but I can't. When I finally catch up, I watch Dad drop at Mrs. Howlman's front door, crying and unnerved. Suddenly the atmosphere becomes hazy and dark and it feels like my body is being sucked backwards. The swing slightly shakes when Mrs. Howlman pulls herself up. She places the picture back in my hand. "After that happened, the town chastised your father. And he and his family left the next week. He promised he'd come back and make things right. I told him he didn't have to because I knew what he told me was the truth." Mrs. Howlman smiles softly. I'll go make us some tea." She pats my thigh and goes inside. Zev thinks my dad let his parents die and he was too scared to try and save them. He doesn't understand what really happened. Zev needs to know, I have to tell him.

Chapter 19

Mom pushes the cart to the car and carefully slides it into the back seat. She cleaned the entire living room and two bathrooms and I, surprisingly, completely cleaned the back porch. I removed all the cobwebs, scrubbed the floors, and even the walls. I resituated the furniture and sanded away most of the rust off the arms and legs. I was cleaning hard and at top speed, mostly I was fueled from my freaky trip down memory lane. While I was cleaning I was waiting for Zev to pop up so I can explain to him about his parents and Aja. Not that he would believe me but it would be worth a try. But, of course, he never showed up again. I slide into the passenger seat as my mom starts the car. It's extremely dark when we're leaving Mrs. Howlman's house. Mom pulls out of the driveway at a slow pace. "Wow, we got a lot of cleaning done. You should come with me more often." She grips the steering wheel and yawns. "It's been a long day." I agree, looking out into the dark atmosphere. Mom yawns again, her eyes completely shut. The car slightly swerves. "Mom, are you sleepy? Maybe I should drive." "No, no I'm fine." Mom opens her eyes wide and straightens her back as much as her body will allow. "See, I'm fine." Her stomach slightly rumbles as she rubs it. “Mrs. Howlman is a very nice lady but her food just doesn’t look good. We definitely have to pack our own lunch. It’s not good to go that many hours without eating.” Mom’s right, I’m starving. I chew my gum slower trying to savor the cherry flavor. “I know it’s late but when we get home I’m going to cook us steak and you can toss a green salad. Doesn’t that sound good? ” Ugh, not really. Mom never cooks rice or bakes cornbread like dad used to. It’s too fattening she says. Mom’s eyes are focused on the road as her lids begin to slowly close. I can feel myself doing the same. In between sluggish blinks I see someone brightened by the headlights. “Mom?!” She snaps out of her drowsiness and quickly swerves to avoid a pedestrian collision. The car spins downward into the woods. We’re both screaming and trying to brace ourselves against whatever impact will be made. The headlights shine the path to our fate as the car crashes into a large tree trunk. My body is thrown forward and my forehead smashes into the dashboard. The blaring car horn becomes muted as blackness engulfs me.

☽

I slowly open my eyes to a dark pewter sky and heavy clouds. Am I dead? “Well, look who’s awake?” Aja stands over me and pulls me up by arms. I grimace, releasing a yell. “I’m sorry, are you hurt?” She clenches my swollen, cut forearm, digging her thumbnail into the wound. I close my eyes tight and chew my lower lip till its bloody, trying to curb the pain. She laughs and lets my arm loose. “Aja what are you doing?” Zev is honestly confused as he grabs her arm and drops a blanket and basket. “I’m just finishing what we started at the cabin; our plan to make Lia pay for how her father abandoned yours on that night…when he died.” She plucks his chin. “No! You told me we were going to have dinner and you bring me here for this? I told you I’m going to let it go.” He looks at my painful disposition. “You said if I stopped talking to her, you wouldn’t hurt her.” “I did say that, but saying and doing are two different things." She smiles and disgustingly, Zev looks away. "She still hasn't woken up." Aja crouches over my mom, whose lying on her stomach, and pulls her head up by her hair. "Let go of her." My tone becomes serious. Aja lets mom's face drop back onto the rock-strewn dirt and as a result a faint cracking sound is made. "You told me to let her go." She laughs and swiftly scales up a large-trunked tree "I had no idea jumping in front of a car would cause an accident like that." She laughs and grabs hold of a branch with her legs. "That was you!" Instantly she's standing so close to me the tips of our noses are touching. "Yeah that was me" her green eyes burn amber "what are you going to do about it?" "You don't scare me. I know your secret." "Really, and what's that Lia?" Condescendingly, she twists the tip of my ponytail with her fingers. "You're a half-breed, too." Her eyes widen with anger and my next instance is to punch her in her jaw. Her entire head twists to the left as droplets of blood fly from her lip. Zev kneels down next to Aja. "What is she talking about?" I rush over to my mom and turn her on her back. "Mom, mom wake up." I softly pat her cheek. Aja quickly recovers and drops onto me causing us to tumble into a position that's a disadvantage for me. She sits on my stomach, pressing her knees into my sides and rams her fists into my chest. "You don't know anything about me!" She depresses her forearm against my neck. I can feel my air passage being blocked. I try to push her off and it makes her choke me harder. Through blurry vision I can see a long raised scar stretching the length of her elbow and up the back of her arm. "I'm going to make you disappear like the rest of them. I'll make everybody pay for the horrible life I lived. My mother slept with a Seeker, is that any reason for her fellow "wolf brethren" to kill her. Huh? This is some community. " She applies more pressure to my neck. "And then my dad, who loved me so much, I watch him get his heart ripped out by YOUR father." I grip my fingers around a rough rock. "One by one I'm going to lead each and every wolf to their death." Devilishly, she smiles and lowers her tone to a whisper. "Do you want to go next or should it be Zev?" I bang the rock into the side of her head, temporarily giving me time to try an escape. My mom slowly sits up, still dazed. Panicky, I crawl over to her and tightly hug her. "Mom, we have to go. We have to get out of this town, now." "Amelia, what's going on?" "Okay it's too much to explain, but Zev told me some things, I've seen some things and it all makes sense." "What does, Amelia?" She brushes some leaves from her shirt. "Dad and this entire town are all wolves, everybody…including me." Mom pulls away from me. "Amelia, you're talking crazy." "It's the truth!" I try to convince her while pulling her up. "Stop it, Amelia! Your father was a hard worker, a good husband, and father. He wasn't a "werewolf". They're not even real." I totally ignore the last comment and continue with my quest of persuasion. "Did you know about dad? His history or where he came from?" Her mind races for an answer she can't find and we really don't have time to wait for one. "Mom please, it's too much to explain right now but we have to go." As soon as she stumbles to her feet, a morphing Aja, leaps onto my mom's back forcing her to fall to the ground. "Going somewhere?" She roars. Mom screams while turning her face away. "What is that?!" She tries to crawl away through the foliage. "I'm the thing that you said wasn't real." Aja smiles and grabs my mom's ankle. "Get away from her." Just as I gained enough courage and strength to fight a stomach cramp wrenches inside of me. "What does she mean "half-breed"?" Zev twists Aja's arm, pulling her away from my mom. Instantly, she turns human, staring into Zev's eyes. He covers her exposed body with his over-sized sweat jacket. "She doesn't know what she's talking about." She says sweetly, turning on her charm. "Ask her how she got that scar on her elbow Zev. Ask her." I plead with Zev to ask her about her scar. "How'd you get it?" Zev asks. Aja doesn't answer. "Tell me how you got it!" "I was pushed." She softly fingers the lifted scar. I finish the explanation. "By my dad, when he jumped on top of a Seeker, Aja's father, to save your dad's life." Zev narrows his eyes as Aja chews on her lip in attempt to subdue her anger. "Your dad was a wolf hunter?" She slightly turns away. "Well, was he?!" Zev grabs her elbow, snapping her body closer to his. "Yes." Aja snatches away and rubs her elbow. "You lied to me! You told me he was sick at home." "Did you honestly think I was going to tell you the truth?" Aja laughingly replies. The full, shining moon seems to glow in the darkening sky. I lay flat on the ground in writhing pain and it feels like I'm burning from the inside out. I dig my fingernails into the earth as I can feel my body contorting and coiling. I look at my bursting finger tips as my nails begin to thicken and sharpen. My body continues to wither with pain as it excruciatingly expands, causing my clothes to burst at the seams. Zev drops to my side and softly strokes my hair. My mom is pressed against a tree staring at me like I'm a monster. "Mom." I call to her, reaching my hand out. She turns her face away and tightly closes her eyes. Aja stands over me and smiles. "Poor thing, she can't handle her morph. It must be killing her. Let's hope it is." "Enough Aja!" Zev demands. "You've been lying to me this whole time. You didn't help me at the cabin because I was upset with Lia. You did it because you wanted payback for yourself. She didn't do anything wrong, I never should have put her in that situation." Zev kisses my forehead. "I'm sorry for everything." He whispers. "I know it hurts at first but it won't after awhile." "Zev, you don't understand what's it's like to be half-breed." Aja insists. The Seekers are my uncles, my family. I stay loyal to them and they'll stay loyal to me." Even in pain I can see the phony emotion behind her reason. "That's why I had to do the things I did." I see her slide a knife from the picnic basket. "She's the killer." I painfully mouth. Zev reads my lips as he comes to an instant realization. "It was you?" He shouts, turning to face her, forcing her to quickly hide the knife against the side of her thigh. "It was me, what?" Aja laughs pretending like she's completely confused.

"Where are they?" "Who are you talking about Zev?" "Tay and Sammy!"

Chapter 20

"They are where they should be." She takes small, slow steps toward him. "Along with Daniel," she happily smiles at me "Jojo, and where you'll be going next." Aja retracts the knife in the air and rushes Zev. He darts out of her path and gracefully transforms. Not like me, confined to the ground, filled with the horrible sensation of a stabbing death. When is it over? God, please make it stop. The moon is at its brightest, it seems like it's positioned directly over me. Aja and Zev circle each other, his chocolate coat shining under the moonlight. Mom takes this opportunity and slowly moves towards me. "Honey, what's happening?" She extends her hand to rub my arm and instead pulls away. I can't tell if she is more horrified or disgusted. "Mom, you should go?" My low-tone sounds loud in the quietness. "I don't want to leave you." Tears glide down her cheeks and despite her revulsion she hugs me tight. "Go Mom, I don't want you to get hurt." She hugs me again. "I love you, Lia." My eyes meet hers in surprise and she smiles softly before darting into the trees. I turn over on my stomach, weakly lifting my upper body using my forearms. Aja looks crazier than I remember as she eyes Zev and makes dog whistles. "Come here doggy." She taunts him with the blade of the knife, striking it through the air. Zev swiftly bites and retracts, leaving teeth marks and streams of blood on her bare thigh. She howls in pain and grabs her thigh. "That was stupid of you to do." She looks down at her bitten thigh. "I was thinking about letting you live." Her joker-like smile shows her pointed, lengthy teeth. "Now I guess I'll have to kill you." I'm standing now, wobbly and unbalanced. Her eyes dart to me "after I kill your girlfriend." That comment gains my full attention and I watch her, quickly, push Zev over the cliff. His claws are scrambling to hold onto the rocky edges. Aja begins shouting. "I knew that Zev liked you from the beginning. I tried to psyche myself out but it was too late, it was obvious. And I used to wonder how he could like a half-breed? Zev's always quoting wolf brotherhood this and stick to our own kind that, let's remain pure and protect the breed. And yet look who he adores." She's calmly walking toward me, tapping the tip of the knife's blade against her temple. I'm frozen in this spot. My brain is telling me to move but my body isn't corresponding. "He tried to kill you, Lia. But he just couldn't. I guess new found love got in the way." I begin to panic and take a step backward. "Today, you won't be so lucky. I would morph and kill you on impact, but that wouldn't be fair, now would it? Look at you, you're stuck in-between. Even in morphing, you're half and half." She laughs at her own joke and holds the reflecting blade in the air. "See? Hideous I know." I look at her and then at the blade. Half of me morphed-- one eye is larger than the other and shining amber, my skin is thick and hairy, even one of my nostrils has taken on the snout of a wolf, and my fangs are piercing my lip. "Mommy didn't even want to touch you." She makes sad eyes and pouts her lips. She's right, I'm hideous. No wonder my mom was acting that way. Aja softly smiles at my awed demeanor. Even though I look this way I can't let her mind games distract me. I step back and the heel of my foot hangs over the edge. Unbalanced, I wildly flap my arms in an attempt to gain footing. Just when I can feel gravity winning, she grabs my arm. "I can't let you die that way, that'll be no fun." She yanks my arm forward with the knife raised in the air. Although I know I'm probably going to die, I don't give up. I fight as hard as I can. I'm not a world champion boxer but I get a few punches in good enough to bloody her nose and split her lip. And still it's like nothing fazes this psycho. She begins to laugh as she wipes the blood from her nose, her eyes begin burning golden. I throw a couple more punches, I even try a couple of kicks and instead of defeating her and winning my gaudy golden waist belt, I'm only tiring myself out. "You're getting tired, already? Too bad, I was starting to have fun." She slings her fingers around my neck and squeezes so tight I think my eyeballs are going to burst. "Hold still." She lifts the knife and the tip of the blade is going to pierce through the center of my chest when she's knocked to the side. Zev's on top of her, both of their bodies are hanging over the edge of the cliff. Aja struggles with him, ripping off chunks of fur and in return Zev bites her skin off her shoulder. Then it happens, almost simultaneously, I see her position the blade to stab Zev in his side and I feel my body change completely. The pain is completely gone. I'm on all fours, fully-fanged, and I feel liberated to defend Zev. But it's too late. Aja slides the dripping bloody blade out of Zev's side. She smiles at me as she wipes the blade clean using his fur. Fueled by infuriation, I don't even realize when I jump off the cliff and grip my fangs around her neck. A snapping sound is made as her tendons break and her head disconnects from her neck. I swing my hind legs forward till I'm back on the ground. I drop her head and it rolls to the side, embedded with a look of surprise. He falls to his back on a safer place of the cliff and turns into the Zev I recognize. I turn back too. I pull the hoodie off Aja and drape it over Zev. I press my hands against his side and a heavy continuous blood stream is seeping through my fingers. "Zev?" I tearfully rub his cheek. "Don't leave me." I lay next to him, resting my head on his chest and pulling the hoodie to cover both of us. I can hear his heart beating. It thumps slower and slower. "I won't" I sit up quickly. "Zev!" He smiles weakly and cautiously stands keeping his hand over his wound. Slowly, he pulls on his torn jeans. "I thought you died." "I would if you hadn't have saved me." Embarrassed, I look down and beamishly smile. "That was some crazy, air borne, wolf fighting. It was pretty good…for a half-breed." My amber eyes quickly meet his with confusion and anger. The camber of his eyes and his gentle smile compliment his tease. He pulls me against him and squeezes my waist with his forearms. His fingers find the small of my back." I'm honestly sorry for everything that happened. You didn't deserve any of it…" Zev begins to apologize. I don't even entirely hear his admission of guilt because the feelings of compassion, eagerness, and excitement gush throughout my body and I go into my own little world with Zev, marriage, and a baby carriage. Okay, well, maybe not the baby carriage yet. I love him. I know I do. But I can't say it. I think it's too soon. I don't want to scare him. "I love you." He says it with a peck on the lips. Huh? I'm in complete shock. I say it back now, right? Of course I do. "I love you too." "It took you long enough." He laughs while arching his side. I firmly press my hand against his wound "come on, let's get you some help." I grab hold of his arm, helping him walk.

CHAPTER 21

It's already been two years since my morph. I sit on the window seat watching giant raindrops explode onto the windowsill. It's a dark day, like always. Heavy clouds, gray skies, willowing trees, and muddy paths are my constant atmosphere. And it's what I've grown used to. I used to hate being here but I realize that Wolf Falls is where I belong, with my own breed. I guess my mom felt the same way. I've never seen her again since that day on the cliff. And if I didn't need her before, I really need her now. I pull my knees against my chest and wrap my arms around my calves. Even though I feel this way, I know that I'm not alone because there's an entire community like me. But sometimes, still, it's lonely. I wish my dad was here with me. There are so many things I could have learned from him. Like how to control my senses, what weakens me, and what strengthens me. As I try to impossibly count all the falling raindrops, a hooded man walks past the window. He feels me watching and turns. I begin to choke from disbelief. "Dad?" I mouth. He continues to stare. "Happy Birthday, Lia." I jump turning to Zev as he kisses me. "Did I scare you?" He quickly smiles and scoops some frosting off the sprinkled cupcake. I turn back to the window and he's gone. "What's wrong, Lia?" Zev's eyebrows furrow in concern. "Nothing, I thought I saw someone." "Who, one of those Wolfen? Zev pulls back the curtains and peers through the window. "No." I pull the curtains closed. "That pack's bad for us, Lia. The Seekers already hate us. The Wolfen are making it worse by killing innocents and gloating about it." "Zev" I attempt to interrupt. "How are we supposed to rise and practice wolf brotherhood, if they're pulling us down." He intently looks into my eyes. "Lia," he whispers "me and about ten others are planning on taking the Wolfen out along with the Seekers. I need to know if you're going to be down…" Mrs. Howlman interrupts when she walks into the room holding a small white box. "You're going to be doing what?" She walks closer to the window seat. "Nothing." Zev chews on the inside of his lip and strokes his hand over his cropped hair. Two signs that he needs to tell me something important. "Happy Birthday, Lia." She smiles softly, fine wrinkles crease around her eyes. "Thank you." I grin and quickly pull the top off. Instantly my grin flat lines with surprise and embarrassment. I hold up a tiny, pale green sleeper. Neatly wrapped underneath is a pair of crocheted pale green and white booties. "How'd you know?" I tear up. "I just do." She tightly embraces me and kisses my forehead. "That doesn't look like it's going to fit her." Zev takes the sleeper and holds it against my chest. "That's because it's not for me." I fold the outfit and lay it back in the box. I've been trying to figure out how to tell Zev for two weeks now and I can't. I just get so nervous. We've never talked about kids, I don't even know if he wants them. Well I guess there's only one way to find out. "I'm...um…pregnant." "Huh?" He lifts one eyebrow. "You know, a baby, growing inside here..." I point to my stomach. "…with child, a bun in the oven." "I get it." Zev looks at my stomach then back to my face. "Are you sure?" "Yeah very." His response isn't quite what I was expecting. I was anticipating a surprised face, a huge smile, lifting me up in the air, and twirling me around, exactly in that order. "Are you happy?" I ask. "Yes." He shakes his head slowly, leans in, and hugs me, kissing me on my cheek. I softly smile. I guess that's acceptable although I'd rather have had the excited "I'm going to be a father" reaction. "Oh, so what did you want to ask me before I got "my gift"?" I point to the baby outfit. "Nothing, it's not important." He manages a smile and kisses my stomach before going upstairs.

☽

I can't believe it. She's pregnant. What do I do? I'm not ready to be a…father. I lower my body down onto the bed, staring into the ceiling. I have so many things I want to do--I need to do to make The Falls better. I can't do that with a baby. My cell phone buzzes off the small table pulling me from my thoughts. "Hello?" I try to clear my throat. "Zev, man, what's wrong?" "Nothing's wrong. Why?" "You sound startled." "I was…um sleeping." "Oh, sorry 'bout that." "So, what's up, Loch?" "I was just calling to make sure that you were still down for The Falls." "You know I am." "Good, because we need to make sure we have all the muscle we can when we take care of the trash in this place." "Yeah." I solemnly agree. "Even if we die, it's all for the cause of brotherhood." Suddenly I start to think about Lia and a growing stomach. Truthfully, I wasn't worried about dying before. But with the news of a baby, I want to be here to see my child but still I want to be a part of the cause to maintain our brotherhood. I feel so conflicted. "Zev, you there, man?" "Yeah, Loch" I try to push the thought of fatherhood to the shadows of my mind. "Alright so we'll meet in the chambers in an hour, with the others to continue this conversation."I can hear the excitement in his voice. "Okay." I hang up, place the phone back on the table, and press my forehead into my cupped hands. "Who was that?" She startles me. "That was Loch." Lia makes a disapproving face and sits down next to me. "I know that's your friend but he doesn't seem like he's a good influence."

She softly touches my hand. "Ever since that happened with Tay and Sammy, you've been searching for friends. But I don't think you've found a good one in him." She tilts her head forward to look into my eyes. "You don't need to worry." I try to reassure her with a smile. "Everything's going to be fine." I kiss her and stand up. "Where are you going?" She watches me pull on my jacket. "I'll be back." I pull my hood on as soon as I step outside to cover myself against the sheets of falling rain. There are things Lia won't understand. Things I have to change. We are not evil - however there is a pack – that are making The Seekers cross into our territory more than ever, forever "seeking" us. We must always be watchful and ready to fight. Because if a war does begin Lia and my baby, will not be touched. That I promise.

About the Author

Phylly Smith is a 19 year old, college sophomore with an untamed imagination. When she's not writing, she enjoys executing art in all its forms, especially sculpting. Phylly is a California native.